Hustle Him

(A Bankshot Romance Series)

By: Jennifer Foor

©Jennifer Foor – All Rights Reserved

Cover Art By : Wicked Cool Designs – Robin Harper

Check out the other books by Jennifer Foor

(Contemporary Romance)

Letting Go - A Mitchell Family Series Book One

Folding Hearts – A Mitchell Family Series Book Two

Raging Love – A Mitchell Family Series Book Three

Risking Fate – A Mitchell Family Series Book Four

Wrapping Up – A Mitchell Family Series Novella 4.5

Wanting More – A Mitchell Series Book Five

Saving Us – A Mitchell Family Series Book Six (March2013)

Hope's Chance (Contemporary Romance)

The Somnian Series (YA Paranormal)

Books 1-5

Coming Soon

Hustle Him (A Bank Shot Romance Book 2) April 2013

I would like to thank everyone that continues to support me through the good times and the bad. Without you, I would never stay so determined. I never realized how rough things would be when I started to follow my dream of writing. There have been so many nights of microwave dinners and ignoring my family to make these books what they are today.

Beta Readers

Jennifer Lafon, Amy Haigler, Karrie Stewart, Jennifer Harried, Erica Willis, Sarah Thompson, Mechelle Lovell Jackson, Kim Eckley, Kim Person, Milasy Mugnolo, Rebecca Gentes, Heather Gunter and Stephanie Horning

Web Design and Marketing by: Amy Haigler

Thanks to all of my new friends on my FB, Twitter and Goodreads.

Author: Amanda Bennett, Author: Elizabeth Buchanan

Author: Emily Snow Author: Michelle Valentine: Michelle Leighton

Thank you for spreading the word and all of the support you give.

Thanks to all of my other Independent Author Friends.

(you know who you are)

Thank you to all the book bloggers out there spreading the word for me and others who write.

Maryse Book Blog, Into the night Reviews, Book Bitches, Word, Rockstars of Romance, Kindlehooked, Shh Mom's reading, Totally Booked, Word, Reading is my time out, Stick Girl Book Reviews, Wolfels World of Books

Book Broads, Book Studs, Books Books Books, Reality Bites Books, Naughty Mafia Vegas, Smutty Book Whores,

What to read after fifty shades

Special Thanks to:

All of my friends and family. Without them, I wouldn't be anywhere. I love you all.

Chapter 1

Ramsey

"I can't believe it's snowing. Doesn't Mother Nature know that spring started four days ago?"

"Jules, we can't control the weather, babe. You know that. Did you have fun tonight? The Gunderson's seem like good people." My wife hated that I had taken the position and relocated us four months ago. I'd been a cop for ten years now and after working in the city for the last nine of them, we just wanted a slower kind of life.

I liked being on the force and putting away criminals, but where we lived before just wasn't a place to raise a little girl.

"Daddy, when will we be home? Can I have a snack before bed?" My daughter, Katie, usually went to bed at eight. We were nearing eleven and she wasn't exactly her cheerful self.

"About five minutes, sweetheart." I peeked in the rearview mirror at my daughter. She hugged her teddy bear.

My wife, Jules, reached over and put her hand on my thigh. "They were nice people. I think you found the nicest people in the whole town on purpose, so that I would like this place even more."

I looked over at her and smiled. "So, you do like it?"

She shrugged and looked out at the snow. "It's beautiful here. Who wouldn't want a good nights sleep without fire trucks and police sirens every five minutes? The smells of the farms are a little hard to get used to, but it is nice."

I put my hand over hers. "I know you miss your parents."

"It would have been easier if they could have come too," she admitted.

"As soon as they sell off the property, they said they would. The market just isn't moving that fast right now. Besides, you need to seek out the biggest bible thumpers so your mom can fit right in." Sure, I was teasing her. My wife's mother wasn't that bad, but since her kids had all moved out, she became obsessed with the bible channel. The woman literally watched it the entire time she was awake and in her house.

I never had a problem with being a Christian. It was the way I was raised, but this woman drank her rum and Coke at ten in the morning and snuck cigarettes on the back porch, while gossiping to her church friends about what liars the rest of the congregation was. It was extremely disturbing.

Jules could talk about her mother constantly, but the moment I said anything negative she would go ballistic and it would start a huge argument. She claimed that I worshipped my non-drinking mother, but degraded hers. Since I hated arguing with my wife, it was best that I kept my opinions to myself.

We'd been together since we were sixteen years old. She was with me when I decided to go into the police academy. After being on the force for three years, she got pregnant with Katie. Even though times were tough, she stayed in college and got her teaching degree. Since we'd moved, she no longer had to work and could spend all of her time being a mother instead. Julia had a gift for making beautiful cakes and now that she had the time, she started making them for other people. The money wasn't fantastic, but it gave her something to be proud of.

Our new kitchen was the perfect size for her to work in. We'd bought a house that was a hundred years old. The kitchen had been gutted out and was now all done in Amish Mission style cabinetry and granite countertops. I think that Jules was more excited about the kitchen then she was at our wedding.

It wasn't the big bedroom, or the large soaking tub that sold her on the house. It wasn't even the wrap-around porch with swing, or the large great room with the stone fireplace. No, my wife was madly in love with our kitchen.

"Mom said she talked to the Conner's the last time they visited. She says that they may make an offer on that rancher down the road."

"The one with the large, detached garage? Your dad will love that." Her father loved to tinker. He could make anything.

"Yeah. Mom doesn't seem too thrilled, but I think she just wants to get down here and be close to Katie, so she doesn't really care what house they move to. You know she's leaving the only house they ever lived in? It's going to be emotional for her." I think it was also hard for Jules to say goodbye to the house she grew up in.

"Daddy, can we build a snowman when we get home?"

"No!" Jules and I said at the same time.

"Sweetheart, it's way past your bedtime. We can build one in the morning." I knew she would have us up as soon as the sun was rising.

"Do we have a carrot?" she asked.

I looked at Jules and scrunched up my face. She shook her head and started to laugh. "For the nose, silly."

"Oh! I don't know, but even if we don't, I'm sure we can figure out something else to use. Maybe our snowman could have a pickle nose instead."

"Eww! No way! It can't have a pickle nose."

Jules turned around and laughed with Katie. "Daddy has silly ideas, doesn't he?"

I looked back in the rearview mirror and saw my daughter laughing. "Why can't it have a pickle nose? Maybe it might get hungry?"

I loved seeing her smile. It was my reason for life. From the moment that child took her first breath I knew I would never love anything more. She made any bad day forgettable and my heart was always the fullest when she was in my arms. Every time Katie and Jules laughed at my jokes, I felt overwhelmed with self-worth. We'd had tough times through the years, sometimes even fighting to stay together. At the end of the day, I knew that I would never want to be anywhere else.

"Snowmen don't eat pickles, Daddy. They eat snow." Katie laughed even more.

"So they eat their own hands? That's gross!" I teased.

"Daddy!" She continued to giggle.

I looked back at my daughter and then over to Jules. One of my hands still sat over hers. "I love our life, babe. We're going to be so happy here. I promi—"

"DADDY, WATCH OUT!"

It was too late.

I turned to look at the dark road and saw the tractor trailer on its side, sliding right toward us. Out of instinct I slammed on my brakes, causing us to go into an uncontrolled spin. I heard my girls screaming and I started screaming too. The roads were too slick to be able to retain control. I knew it was just a matter of seconds, but for me, it seemed like it played out in slow motion. I tried to turn and look at Jules. Her eyes were huge with fear.

The impact was sudden and I hardly remembered what it felt like that exact moment. The sound of the metal making contact was piercing. I was suddenly cold and looking around to see glass everywhere. My shoulder was stuck to my seat by a large piece of shrapnel that had come off the truck. I tried to jerk myself free except the pain was excruciating.

Realizing that I wouldn't be able to free myself without help, I turned to ask Jules, but there was another large piece of metal in between us. The first thing I noticed was that I didn't hear either of my girls. I called out into the cold air, seeing the truck driver running in the direction of my car.

"Jules? Jules, are you okay, babe? Katie? Katie, answer Daddy. Just tell me what hurts, sweetheart."

Nothing.

I screamed their names, even when the driver came and opened my door. "Get them! Just help them!"

The old man, who looked to be in his sixties, peeked inside of my wrecked car. He pulled off his hat and shook his head, but looked right at my face. "Oh, God, I am so, so sorry. Help is on the way, sir. I've already called."

"Just get them out! Why can't I hear them? Are they conscious?" I had to know. I had to know they were okay. I had to hear my little Katie's voice. She had to be okay. We were two minutes from home.

The old man just stood there shaking his head and trying his best not to look toward the opposite side of my car.

While he just stood there, I called out for them, over and over again, with not a single sound in return.

I don't know how long it was before help arrived. The emergency workers started on my side and I couldn't understand why. I yelled for them over and over again to help the girls. Hell, I knew half of the guys there. Maybe they had gotten out of the car already and they were just on the side of the road getting looked at?

It wasn't until they brought out the Jaws of Life and started cutting me out of my car that I realized the extent of the accident. As my body was pulled away from the wreckage, I looked back and saw why nobody would give me an answer. The entire passenger side of my car was crushed against the steel walls of the truck. As they strapped me down to the gurney, I screamed out for my girls, over and over. This couldn't be happening. It had to be a dream. It had to be…

"Sheriff, can you hear me? Sheriff Towers?"

I looked up from my desk and realized that I'd been daydreaming again. It happened every single day since the accident last year. When I lost my girls, I lost all of my reasons for living. I didn't want to survive that accident. I shouldn't have.

This was my punishment.

I closed myself off from the rest of our family, unable to live with the burden of being the driver that night. I'd killed my girls and I would never be able to forgive myself.

After it all happened, I gave up on working, paying bills, and having a life at all. The bank took the house and with little left in my savings, I moved to West Virginia to a little town where I wouldn't have to talk about what had happened to me. I was sick of the whispers and condolences. Didn't they know that the mere mention of their names brought back every single beautiful moment of our life together? Couldn't they fathom that I didn't want to have to imagine living out a full life and never being able to hear them tell me that they loved me? Did they know what it was like to sleep in my daughter's room and cry like a small child? Had they not considered that every single thing in my life reminded me of my girls? It had become too much to handle.

Making the move was the easiest of decisions. An old friend got me the job and had put in a good word for me. The town was small with only two thousand people. I found a cabin about five miles down a mountainous country road, off the beaten path.

I just wanted to be alone—to be able to live out my life in seclusion. I wasn't an idiot. With the internet out there, it was obvious that some people would know the truth. Still, not one of them had the balls to mention my past to me. I'd rather them fear me, then ask the questions that I would never have been able to answer.

"Sheriff, are you alright?" My deputy, Shelton Morris, asked again.

I shook off the flashback and put on a fake smile. "Yeah, sorry. I was just thinking about something."

"You want to talk about it?" Shelton was a nice kid. He was in his early twenties and his Grandpappy had been the sheriff for forty years before me. He died of a massive heart attack six months ago.

"Nah, it's all good. What were you saying?" I had to keep up the charade that I was just one man. They wouldn't be able to understand what it was like to lose everything. Not one day went by where I hadn't asked myself why I had lived and they had... died.

My girls were in my heart and the flashbacks were enough of a reminder that I had taken their lives. I just wanted to do my job and go home without the stares or the burning questions.

"Listen, I know you're new here, but it ain't good to hold things in. If you ever need to talk, just let me know. You seem like maybe you need a friend. You been here for nearly six months and nobody knows a dang thing about you, 'cept for what they read about. I'm just sayin', if you need a buddy, we can have beer sometime."

I put on a fake smile and stood up from my desk. "I appreciate that. I'm good. Just not real used to the quiet out here. I'm finding it hard to sleep at night." The sleeping part was true, but it wasn't because of the quiet. It was because I was alone. I was a broken man and I couldn't be fixed, not by a therapist, or even a buddy. There was no hope for me.

Shelton shook his head and smiled back. "Alright, man. Well, I need to run out and check on Mrs. Parks. She claims that someone keeps vandalizin' her mailbox."

"That's real crime there." This was what we dealt with in this town. We didn't have gangbangers or drive-bys.

"Yeah, well, it's a job!" Shelton laughed as he walked out the door. I waited for him to leave before standing up and getting another cup of coffee. The flashbacks were worse when I didn't sleep the night before. I usually had bourbon to help with that, but the more I used that as a solution, the less it worked.

This was my life. It was never going to be any better.

Chapter 2

Vessa Jean

Mornings were so hard for me, considering that I was usually up until two, closing out the bar that I bartended at. My life didn't just revolve around my job though; I had two kids that needed to be taken care of. Sure, their dad was around, but between his job doing tattoos at the shop and his outside customers, he wasn't home that much to be able to manage the kids schedules. Not that I expected it out of him either way. He was pretty much worthless when it came to being responsible.

I loved my children. They were my whole world. Asha was ten and Logan was almost six and with their opposite personalities, they were sometimes hard to handle. They fought a lot, making my life even harder at times. Gavin, my husband, was never there to see any of that though.

His parents were still pretty young and had two kids that were in school themselves. My husband happened to be their accidental teenage pregnancy that had led to their twenty-five year marriage. Unfortunately, as much as they loved their grandkids, they were much too busy working and raising their two youngest, Gabe and Gwen. Yeah, they went with all the same letters.

My mother died when I was sixteen of an aneurism, due to complications from a rare form of brain cancer. She was fine when I went to school and by the time I came home she was gone. My father did a pretty good job raising me, but he'd drank himself to death and died of liver failure three years ago. Ever since then, I'd had to depend on myself for everything.

I'd been with Gavin since we were fifteen years old. Our on again-off again relationship through high school was like gasoline to the fire. At times it was downright violent and, for some reason, we both kept coming back for more. When I got pregnant at seventeen, it was pretty much a given that we were going to get married. His parents wanted us to be just like them and, much to our surprise, we had made a pretty good life for ourselves. Granted, we worked our butts off and rarely had time for each other, but what married couple with young children did?

Gavin started doing tattoos when he was twenty-one. He'd always been great at art anyway, so it just made sense. He started working for the current shop he was at about four years ago. An old friend of his started it and added Gavin to the list of artists there. The job was great and the pay was pretty good too, but what happened at the shop was not alright with me.

They had these little groupie chicks in there all the time. They'd just hang out and drink with the older guys that worked there, including my husband. Of course, he liked the attention, and last year, I found out that he'd hooked up with one of them after hours.

It broke my heart.

Every single day I was busy busting my ass trying to help pay the bills and make sure our children were taken care of, while he was out sticking his dick in some little wall banger. It made me sick.

I wanted to leave him, but without my parents and no real friends, I looked at my children and knew that they needed stability. It was bad enough that all of the other kid's parents talked behind our backs because we looked different than them. Gavin had used my arm and other parts of my body as a human canvas. At first, all of my tattoos were easily covered, but after he finished with my sleeve was when I really started to hear the whispers and see the dirty looks. It didn't matter that they were beautiful flowers or my children's names. I looked different and they hated me for it.

I was never asked to go on field trips or to join the PTA. Even when I volunteered for class parties, I was never picked. I knew the reason, but it not only hurt my children, it hurt me too. I was a damn good mother—better than half of the mothers in my children's classes. Still, they saw what they wanted in me and never gave me a chance otherwise. My husband and I had tattoos. I had my nose pierced.

So what?

I had the same problem with finding a job. Even after taking a bunch of college courses online after my first child was born, people just wouldn't hire me for anything that had to deal directly with the public. I ended up borrowing money from my father to complete a bartending course. It worked out to benefit me more in the long run. I had a great clientele and made pretty good money doing it. Plus, half of our town ended up at the bar at night.

In the past six months, I hadn't been seeing eye to eye with my husband. For some reason, he wanted me home all the time. I was registered on two pool leagues that I shot on during the time I was working. If the league fell on my day off, I would still show up to be able to socialize and not have it be part of my job. I didn't have real friends, none that I would call trustworthy, that is.

The problem was that I'd met them all from working in the bar. Getting to know someone at that kind of place isn't exactly a good thing. Most people that come into a bar alone are there because they have problems that they want to drink away. I'd heard every kind of story and at the end of the day my team consisted of two town drunks, a seventy-year-old farmer that lost his wife to cancer, and three brothers that were more focused on who could get laid the fastest each week.

My husband, who I had been in love with since puberty, didn't understand why I needed a social life outside of work. He felt that my line of work was the only socializing I would ever need. In fact, he said my real job was maintaining the town gossip and learning everyone's dirty secrets.

I don't know why he complained. I contributed to our family and managed to make things work. At the end of the day, I loved them and would do anything to make sure they never had to need for anything.

It wasn't until this past winter that things really started to fall apart. I'd noticed Gavin was being distant. He would come home all giddy and want to spend time with the kids, more than usual. I thought maybe he just wanted to be a better father at first. I didn't mind that he was ignoring me for the kids. They were the most important anyway.

As the winter months passed, we communicated less. One night, I sat him down and told him how I felt. He blamed it all on me and my guilty conscious, claiming that I wasn't going to let his one indiscretion go.

I wanted to forget, but I also wanted to believe that I was still a desirable woman. I had needs and he just wasn't fulfilling them. One day I went and talked to his mother for a few hours. She suggesting that I give him his space and maybe he was just going through a 'man stage'.

I got back into the rhythm of my daily routine and tried to brush off my suspicions.

One morning, after getting the kids up and ready for school, I started to feel lousy. As the day progressed, so did my health. I called work and let them know that I wouldn't be able to come in. Since I rarely ever took a day off, they were great about it and wished me well. I took some cold medicine and went straight to bed.

When I woke up, got the kids off the bus, and finally got started on dinner, Gavin was walking in the door. Right away he noticed that I wasn't dressed for work. "What's wrong with you? You know you're going to be late?"

"I called out sick." I stirred the pot of soup and didn't look up at him.

"That's just great! You get a damn stuffy nose and suddenly can't work. Pathetic!" I heard him turn around and head out of the kitchen. His words hurt me. Even when I was sick, I still did everything I needed to do. His lack of compassion rubbed me the wrong way. Why hadn't he even asked if I was okay, or what was wrong with me?

I walked right into the living room and found him sitting with the kids. "What is your problem? I never call out sick. Don't you even care if I'm okay?"

He laughed but never took his eyes away from the sports channel. "Whatever, Ves. You're obviously fine if you are up in my shit about it. How much longer before dinner is ready?"

I put my hands on my hips. I knew that I could cry or I could get pissed. We'd been together way too long for me to be okay with the way he was acting. "You're the one with the problem! I'm sick and you're busy treating me like crap. Wow! I'm so glad that you don't give a damn about me or my health. What would you do if I just dropped dead like my mother did? Would you even care?"

Tears filled my eyes immediately after mentioning her. I missed her so much and it was days like this that I needed her the most.

I made my way into the kitchen and leaned against the countertop to regain my composure.

Hands wrapped around my waist and I felt Gavin breathing against my ear. "I'm sorry. I had a shitty day and told some of the guys they could come over and watch the game tonight. I didn't mean to be a dick to you."

I turned around and looked into his eyes. "Sometimes I feel like you don't even care about me anymore. It's like you don't even consider my feelings."

He frowned in a joking kind of way. "I'm sorry." His hand slid up the back of my shirt. Right away, it gave me the shivers. When he reached my bra line, I gasped and leaned back on the counter.

"Am I still attractive to you?" I knew I wasn't ugly. In fact, I got hit on all the time. After having two kids, I had nice curves, but was still petite and pretty thin. My hair was long, halfway down my back, with different colored blonde streaks through it. I didn't have wrinkles and my breasts didn't sag. I could spend minimal time in the bathroom and feel good about myself.

He kissed the side of my head and pulled me into his arms. "Of course you are."

I slid my hands up the back of his shirt and pulled his warm body against mine. "You never want to spend time alone anymore. Is there someone else?"

He pulled away and started to walk out of the room, before turning to point right at me. "I can't believe you went there—again." He shook his head and then rubbed his face. "Look, I know you don't feel well. I'm just going to call my friends and see if we can hang at one of their houses instead."

Okay? I guess I pissed him off again. Maybe it was always my fault that he avoided me. He could tell me that his cheating meant nothing, but it didn't hurt any less. I felt like if I was doing my job being a wife, then he wouldn't have had to do it in the first place. Maybe if I had my mother to talk to, she could have told me what to do. It wasn't like his mother was ever going to be on my side.

I watched Gavin walk all the way outside into the cold, dark night to make his phone calls. It seemed weird to me, but since I'd already pissed him off about my trust issues, I knew it wasn't a good time to accuse him of being secretive again. Still, I stood at the window and watched his body language. He was all smiles and even laughing at times. I turned away from the window when I saw him hanging up.

He came right inside and walked past me. "It wasn't a problem. I'm just going to head out."

I just stood there, still thinking about how happy he seemed to be talking to his friends. He never looked at me that way. I don't think he would have smiled at me unless I'd fallen on my face. It just rubbed me the wrong way.

What also bothered me was the fact that he'd put on cologne to go play cards with the guys. I considered saying something, but knew it would just cause a tremendous fight between the two of us. As he was walking out, he leaned over and kissed me on the cheek. "Try to go to sleep when the kids do. You look tired."

I expected an 'I love you', except he didn't offer it.

There was definitely something wrong if he would rather be with his friends, than home with his family. Sick or not, I still required some love and understanding. Against his threats, I decided to internet search sites about cheating. I'd only caught him the last time because the girl he was seeing was the mother to one of my children's friends, who we happened to know since we were in grade school. It didn't just rip my heart to shreds. His actions humiliated me.

Why was it so hard for him to dedicate himself to our family? What was I doing wrong?

For the next couple of days I did everything in my power to do nice things for my husband. I'd even gone and gotten some new underwear and planned a romantic evening between the two of us. With Gavin's mother on board, I had a babysitter for the night.

After I dropped them off and came home, I showered and put on only my new bra and panties. I felt sexy and spent an extra few minutes really dolling myself up. I was excited. We hadn't had a night alone in so long. I just wanted it to be perfect.

Gavin usually came home around six. By that time, I'd had dinner done and was just waiting for him to walk in the door. It may have looked ridiculous, but I sprawled myself across the couch, trying my hardest to look seductive.

I wasn't sure what time it was at first, but I woke up when I heard the back door opening. I stretched out my arms, realizing that I'd fallen asleep waiting for him. I straightened up the little bit of fabric I had on and walked into the kitchen.

Gavin was standing over the table, eating with his hands. He cocked an eyebrow when he saw me walk in wearing only underwear. "It's nearly seven. I've been waiting for you."

"Where are the kids and why aren't you wearing any clothes?" He continued shoving the meat into his mouth.

"They're at your mother's for the night. I planned a nice night for us." I put my hands on my hips, expecting him to react to what I had on.

He reached over and grabbed a roll and took a bite out of it. Then he pointed down at the table. "You made this for us? It tastes pretty good."

Pretty Good? "Where have you been? You could have called."

"I was at the shop. We had people there, Vessa. I couldn't just come home and leave them there. It's bad for business." He grabbed another roll and started to walk past me. "I'm getting a shower."

I reached up and caught his arm. "Wait! I made this food for us to enjoy. Do you even notice what I'm wearing?"

He looked me up and down and shrugged. "Is it new or something?"

I was starting to get pissed. "Seriously? I am standing here half naked and you want to know if it's new? Do I not look sexy to you?"

He laughed at me and started shaking his head. "Jesus Christ, Vessa. I worked all damn day and you're going to start on me the second I walk in the door? You look nice, but I'm tired and you never told me you were doing any of this shit. I can't read your damn mind."

I felt defeated. No matter what I did to try to sway him back into romance, I failed.

Instead of following him into the bathroom, I changed into a pair of yoga pants and a tank top and sobbed on the couch. Gavin never even came back out. I heard him snoring a while later and then cried some more. I suppose it would have been easier if I had my mother to talk to. I just wanted to feel like someone loved me.

For the next week, I continued to work hard on getting Gavin to want me. Each night he came home and ignored me. After five days, I'd pretty much given up all hope. I looked forward to going to work and being out of the house for a while.

Unfortunately, when I got to the bar the plumbing had busted. Two inches of water was all over the floor. The owner was standing outside on his phone. He put his hand over it and looked right at me. "You may as well go home for the day, Vessa. The repair guy can't get here until after five. I'm just going to stay closed."

"You sure you don't need my help?"

"Yeah, take a day for yourself. I can handle this shit here."

I climbed back in my car and started to go home. Since it had been a while since I'd been to the shop, I decided to stop by and see Gavin. For the most part they worked by appointments only, so it was important that I not disturb him during a session. I'd hate to be the reason someone walked around with the wrong name on their arm.

They never had anyone working the front counter, but there was a girl standing there. She had her lip pierced and had some kind of flower going across her neck. Her clothes were all black, very tight and very revealing. She flipped her dark hair back away from her face. "Are you here for a tattoo or piercing?"

I laughed and shook my head. "I'm Gavin's wife."

She seemed shocked. "Oh..Um, let me go get him for you."

I grabbed her arm. "It's fine. I know where to find him."

"He's with a client, I think. Let me just go check." She seemed adamant, and I didn't want to make him mad, so I stood still while she rushed by me.

Gavin came out but never smiled when he saw me standing there. "Hey, babe, what are you doing here?" he asked under his breath.

I don't know what it was, but I got the feeling that he didn't want me there. I wanted to know why and I was going to find out. If that bastard was cheating again, I wasn't going to sit around forgiving him.

Chapter 3

Ramsey

As the months went by, there seemed to be no way out of reliving that night. I was haunted every single minute that I was breathing. I didn't know what I'd done to deserve such torture, but couldn't see a way out of it.

My job was mundane in my little old town, but it put food on the table and kept my whiskey bottle full. Maybe if things were different, I would be able to move on. I still missed them so much. I missed the way Jules' hair smelled when she climbed into bed after her shower. I missed the way I never had any covers, because my daughter had climbed into bed between us and wrapped herself up in them. Then there was their beautiful smiles and the way they both told me they loved me; the way they showed me they loved me.

They didn't deserve to die. I didn't deserve this solitary life that I was being forced to live in. I'd rather be dead than to feel this emptiness every day for the rest of my life.

There was one thing that made me focus on something else other than my girls. Ever since I was in the academy, I'd grown to have a love for the game of billiards. I wasn't the best there was, but I was a damn good shot. To keep my personal life separate from being the sheriff, and not allowing anyone in my small town to pry, I would drive a town over to shoot a good game and walk away with a few more, or sometimes a few less, dollars in my pocket.

It may have been temporary, but it took my mind off it all.

The bartender was named Sue. She looked to be in her mid-sixties and had a smoker's cough that you could hear just about every ten seconds. I was positive the woman had emphysema, although she never claimed to be sick. "You want the usual, Ramsey?"

"Yeah, that'll be great." She poured a Jack and Coke and added some ice, before sliding it across the bar.

I looked into the rear part of the bar where the pool tables sat. On any given night, a new set of players were available. This little bar was located on a stretch of road that truck drivers frequented. It had pretty good food and there wasn't another place for miles.

Two bigger guys were already back there shooting against each other. I leaned back against the bar and kept watching them. Sue leaned over so she didn't have to yell. "They've been here since three this afternoon. If you want an opponent than I suggest you head over there now, before they can't even hold the sticks."

I looked back and saw her wink at me. She didn't know my story, but I think that bartenders had a way of reading people. She knew something had happened to me, but at the same time, she never asked what it was.

Sue also knew that I was the sheriff of another town. When strangers got rowdy and I was around, I made sure they left her establishment. She was just a little old lady that didn't need that kind of trouble. Occasionally, she had asked me to come over to her house to help her out when things weren't working. Since she'd lost her husband a while back, she didn't really have anyone else.

"Let me see if I can get a couple games out of them." I grabbed my glass and walked over toward the two guys.

They were both typical truck driver-looking guys. Both had beards and large stomachs from eating on the road all the time. It was a force of habit for me to study the details of people. The dude with the lighter hair wore a wedding ring, where his buddy did not. Usually, but not always, married men were a little harder to sway into playing for money. Most were already treading water when it came to keeping their wives happy. It wasn't easy to be gone all the time.

I looked toward his friend and took another sip of my drink. "You up for a little competition?"

They looked at each other before turning their attention back to me. "What do you have in mind?"

"I was thinking twenty a game." I sat my drink down and pulled a house cue off the wall.

"You some kind of shark?" the married guy asked.

I chuckled. "Hell no! Just like playing for a reason."

His buddy grabbed the balls on the table and started putting them into the rack. "Let's play for ten."

I pulled a coin out of my pocket and held it out under the pool table light. "Flip for the break? Heads or tails?"

"Heads."

The coin flew into the air and landed on the felt of the table. Once it was done spinning, we leaned in to see the result of the flip. It landed on tails, giving me the break, so I grabbed the cue ball and lined it up to break out all the balls.

The break was always the most important shot. It could make or break the game. Luckily, I made two balls and was able to make another four before giving the guy his first shot. I was no pro, but I knew how to hide a ball to prevent my opponent from being able to make a good shot.

I won my first ten easily, but as the games continued, I was still up only ten dollars, after losing a few then winning some more. By the time I started getting tired, and my friends for the night got drunker, I was up a whopping twenty bucks. I shook hands with both of the men and handed Sue my winnings. She hugged me and waved as I headed out.

Morning would come fast and I knew that I hadn't had enough drinks in me to be able to sleep.

My little cabin in the woods was so far off the beaten path that late at night even I had trouble finding the driveway. I'd thought about putting some reflectors out, but I kind of liked the idea that if I couldn't find my place, nobody else could either.

Once inside, I threw my keys down on the table and headed into the kitchen for a beer. On most nights I just slept right in my recliner. There was no sense of even having the four bedrooms the place had. I kept the doors closed and only went into my room to shower and change. After being married and sharing a bed for so long, I hardly moved from my side of the bed. Waking up and seeing that empty spot was just too much to take every damn day.

I must have fallen asleep shortly after getting comfortable. When I woke up, my phone was ringing on the table. I wiped the sleep out of my eyes and got up to answer it.

This is Sheriff Towers.

Sorry to call you so early, Sheriff, but we got a big wreck out on the main highway. I hated when my deputy called me with that information.

How bad is it? I couldn't go if there was a fatality. I just knew I couldn't.

A mother and a couple kids were hit by a tractor trailer headin' out of town, sir. The driver of the truck was unharmed. He said he must have fallen asleep at the wheel and crossed over the double line. The ambulance is on its way for the mother. She's breathin', but isn't responsive. The kids seem to be more shaken up, but I'm goin' to have them sent out to get checked out too. Since I need to stay here at the scene, I'm goin' to need you to transport the kids.

I'm on my way. Text the coordinates.

The whole time I was putting on my boots and getting myself together, I knew that being around children was going to be hard. If the mother didn't survive, it would be my job to tell those kids.

I was in the wrong line of work.

The scene of the accident was chaotic. I spotted my deputy leaning down to talk to two little kids. My first thought was my girls and how I wished that we hadn't been on the road that night. The little boy turned and looked right at me. I took a deep breath and approached them.

My deputy stood up and looked right at me. "I was able to locate the victim's cell phone and use it to contact the last number she called. They were on their way to a family member's house to stay. The aunt is goin' to meet us at the hospital. I let her know that the children are alright, but we just want them to get checked out for precautionary reasons."

The kids were wrapped in one of the blankets that we carry in our trucks, in case of emergencies. They both were looking right at me. Being around kids was so difficult for me. It only reminded me of my sweet little girl that I would never be able to hold again. I sighed and gained enough composure to do my job. "We're going to take a ride now."

The little boy's eyes got big. "In your police truck?"

"Yes."

"Can we use the siren? I bet it's real loud." He was obviously too young to understand that this was a serious situation.

"Sure, kid." I waited for him and his sister to stand up and follow me over to my vehicle.

The little guy was busy looking around the front of the vehicle at all of the gadgets, while his sister remained quiet with her hands folded on her lap. When I went to make sure they were both buckled, she grabbed my hand. "Is my mommy going to be okay?"

It was heart-wrenching to hear her asking. I honestly had no idea if their mother was going to make it. All I knew was that these two children were depending on me to be the hero and I didn't know if I was capable of even having a conversation with them. "As soon as I hear something, you will be the first to know."

"Mom said that we were going to love our new life. I hate this place. I hate that Mommy is hurt. I just want to go home. I want my daddy!" the little boy cried.

I clenched my jaw as I started on our way to the hospital. The more I tried to not think about my own accident, the more I couldn't get it out of my head. By the time we pulled up at the emergency room doors, I had played out the entire scene once again in my head.

We no sooner made it into the emergency room doors when I saw a familiar face heading in our direction. Sue, the owner of the bar I frequented, came over and bent down in front of the kids. She pulled them in for hug and looked up at me. "Thanks for bringing them here, Ramsey… ah… Sheriff."

"You know these kids?" Sue never mentioned grandchildren, but then again, I never asked about anyone's business when mine was locked up from anyone knowing.

She patted the boy on the head and stood up. Her cough was intense. "These kids are my great niece and nephew. Their mother was my sister's only daughter. She passed a while back and we lost touch. I got a call yesterday that she was in trouble and needed to start over. She's the only family I got left and I ain't about to turn my back on her." She grabbed my arm and pulled me to the side. "They're worried about swelling around the brain. These poor kids don't even know me. How am I supposed to tell them she may not wake up?"

I put my hand on Sue's shoulder. As much as I wanted to go home and forget about these people, I knew I wouldn't be able to abandon someone when they needed help. It was all I had ever wanted to do. This woman needed to survive. "Why don't you take the kids and get them checked out, then take them home? I will have someone bring all of their things from the car to your house. If it will make you feel better, I will stay here until we know something more about your niece."

She wrapped her arms around me, taking me back to the funeral of my wife and child, where everyone wanted to hug and console me. I pulled away without even realizing how cold it seemed. I could tell that she knew I had withdrawn from her. She put on a fake smile and held her hands out for both children. "I will be waiting for your call, Ramsey. You're a good man. I hope you know that."

I stood and waited for the woman and the two kids to walk in the direction of triage. The last thing I wanted to do was be involved in something so emotional. Sure, I'd been there before and could probably be great in dealing with pain and grief, except I hadn't been able to let go enough to use my experience for others. Sometimes, I didn't even know if I wanted to.

After grabbing a coffee, I made my way to the room where the injured mother was located. I could hear the beeps of the machines as I entered. A nurse smiled, recognizing who I was from my uniform. I gave her a nod and sat down in a nearby chair. "How is she?"

She finished writing down something before answering me. "We have her stabilized. Because of the head injury, the doctor is worried about swelling. As of right now, we are just waiting. Her vitals are improving and if we can get through the next twenty-four hours, she has a good chance of fully recovering. It could go either way with a brain injury."

I was afraid to look at the bed, where the mother was lying lifeless. I knew she was breathing, except looking at her put a face to the victim. I couldn't let myself get attached to a case, especially one that was so close to my past.

When the nurse left, I started to get up and request that they contact me if anything changed, except my eyes glanced over at the poor mother fighting to live. Her blonde hair was a mess and dried blood made some spots appear red. She had a bandage over her nose and a stitched up spot over her eyebrow. Even with all of that mess going on, I could tell that she was an attractive woman. Her body was covered up with blankets, but her arm was hanging out enough for me to see the artwork that went from her wrist to her shoulder. It was done well and I continued to stare. I thought about the tattoos on my own body—the ones I got after I lost my girls.

Sadness overwhelmed me again, forcing me to sit back down in the chair. This woman was those kids' mother. I had to know that she was going to pull through. I couldn't just walk away. Something wouldn't let me get out of that chair.

I put my hat over my eyes and leaned back to try to rest. Some would say that prayers were all that could be done. I'd lost faith in that. This woman's will to live was what would decide whether she ever opened her eyes again. I owed it to Sue to stick around and wait.

I'm not real sure how long I'd been sleeping, but I woke to someone touching my arm. I grabbed my hat and placed it back on my head as I sat up straight and looked around for the nurse. Instead, the arm with the tattoos was reaching over to touch me again. I stood up, partly in shock, and looked down at the awake woman. She was struggling for words and I knew what she was going to ask before the words could come out. "You're kids are fine, ma'am. They're with your aunt. You've been in an accident. I'll go get you the doctor."

I rushed out of the room, leaving the woman all alone. As I passed the nurse's station, I alerted them of the patient waking up, and left the hospital.

The woman was going to make it. My involvement was over.

Case closed.

Chapter 4

Vessa

I hated men and everything they stood for. All they'd ever done was lie right to my face. I just wanted a new start. I wanted my kids not to have to see the constant bickering and whatever riffraff their father was going to be bringing home.

He'd made it clear that he didn't want to be a full-time father and now, all of the sudden, he was trying to get them back. I knew it wasn't because he missed them, or even because his mother put him up to it. No. This was about getting back at me.

I knew what I did when I left was wrong. It was a moment of temporary insanity. I'd given that man so many faithful years and in return he was living some secret life right under my nose. How was I supposed to react to something like that?

I guess the shit hit the fan two weeks before I had made the decision to leave town. It had come to my attention that my husband was hiding something from me. It didn't take long for me to decide to catch him red-handed. After he left for work one day, I took the kids to school and went back to his tattoo shop. This time, I didn't go in the front door.

I snuck around the back and followed the sounds of music coming from the other side of the window. It was difficult to see through the tiny cracks of the mini blinds, but I was able to spot Gavin. He was sitting on a cheetah print couch with a little young thing straddling him. She was rocking her body back and forth over him as he grabbed onto her ass.

At first I felt sick from the pit of my stomach. That bastard was going to work and getting laid, while I was at home taking care of our family. My sadness turned to anger and soon it was hard for me to control any of my emotions.

I blame what happened on temporary insanity. I never meant for things to go as far as they had. I surely didn't want to break laws. Things happened that became completely out of my control.

After leaving the tattoo shop, I went straight home. It took me a matter of ten minutes to rip out every single article of his clothing and toss them into a large bin in the back yard. I grabbed a bottle of bleach and doused the clothes with it. When they didn't all turn white right away, I grabbed the bathroom cleaners and dumped them in the bin too.

Still feeling like it wasn't enough, I went into his closet and ripped his pictures out of every single photo album. Then I drove myself right to the bank and withdrew all of our savings. I opened up a new account at a different bank in just my name.

I knew it was going to cause problems. I just didn't care. He'd broken my heart—torn it into a million pieces— and I wanted him to pay. He didn't deserve to be happy. No, I was going to leave him with nothing.

I left the kids at my mother-in-law's house while I sat at the kitchen table, completely naked, waiting for him to come home.

I can't describe the look on his face when he came in that door and expected to get laid.

Instead, as he approached me, I took a bottle of beer and threw it right at him. "Fuck you! Do you see this body? You will never touch this again. I hate you. You're nothing but a liar. I gave you my heart and you ripped it into pieces. You deserve that little slut and whatever diseases she might be carrying."

He put his hands up. "Hold up! What the fuck are you talking about, baby?"

"I saw you, Gavin. I saw you with that little bitch. I know you've been fucking her." I couldn't cry. I wouldn't let him think he'd crushed me. I needed to stay furious.

He put his hands into his face and sank down into the chair. "Vessa… I…"

"Don't, Gavin! There isn't anything you can say to make things better. This was the one thing I said I could never go through again and you did it anyway. Obviously, I meant nothing to you."

He looked up at me and had tears running down his cheeks. "Please don't leave me."

"It's going to take me a few weeks to figure out where I am going to live and how much I can afford on my own. In the meantime, the kids and I will stay here. It's up to you to explain this to the kids. I refuse to be the bad guy here. You did this! You remember that!"

"Vessa, they're going to hate me. I can't tell them."

I pointed right at him. "You should have thought about that when you were sticking your dick into some little hobag! I can't even look at you without wanting to gag. You make me sick!"

I didn't wait for him to reply or get up, before I got dressed and headed out to get the kids. When I walked out the door, I could hear him crying. I'd heard it all before and nothing had changed. He'd cheated again, and this time, I wasn't going to forgive him. My marriage was over.

I took the kids out to dinner, but chickened out when it came to telling them what was happening. This was Gavin's mess and he would have to be the one to break their hearts. I didn't want to come out smelling like roses. I just didn't want to be blamed for something that I didn't do.

Gavin slept on the couch for the next two weeks. Every time he tried to talk to me, I shot him down. Words meant nothing to me. It was actions that mattered. He never even got mad about what I'd done to his clothes or pictures.

I only cried when he wasn't around, and even then, it wasn't as extreme as I would have thought.

It wasn't until I went to work one night, where I finally hit rock bottom.

It was business as usual at first. My regulars were sitting at the end of the bar, complaining about their day. A pool league was getting ready to start and some girls were picking out eighties ballads on the juke box. I started washing a couple glasses and noticed two emo-looking chicks walking into the bar. They looked young and I wasn't about to be fined for serving a minor.

"You got ID?"

They looked at each other and laughed. "We ain't here to drink, bitch!"

I think I was shocked at them calling me a name. Nobody ever disrespected me in the bar. I sat the glass down slowly and looked from one girl to the other. They were both covered in tattoos and piercings and I should have known right away why they were paying me a visit. "You can turn your little asses around and leave, right now!"

"You think you can just dictate Gavin's life?" The chick with the longer black hair started shaking her head as she talked. "He was going to leave you anyway!"

I raised my eyebrow and tried to control the steam that was about ready to start blowing out of my ears. "I guess you got what you want then. Gavin and I are over. You can do whatever you want with him."

The other chick, with the black pixie haircut, stepped forward. "That's just it. He doesn't want to see her anymore, because of what you did. You ruined everything!"

I'd had enough. These girls had a lot of nerve. Without backing away, I looked right at them. "Gavin had responsibilities to not only me, but also his kids. If anyone is at fault, it is him. He had the affair and he knew what the consequences would be. Get your little skank asses out of my bar, now!"

"I'm having his baby!" The long-haired girl cried out.

I shook my head. Sure, I wanted to freak out. I wanted to rip Gavin's dick off and hang it to the town's flag pole. "I guess you got the family you wanted then."

"He wants me to have an abortion. He says that we're through. He's blaming me for losing you." Honestly, the girl looked heartbroken. I couldn't feel bad for her situation. She spread her legs for my husband, knowing damn well what his situation was.

"Look, you made this bed and now you have to lay in it. This is what happens when you sleep with a married man."

"Fuck you!"

"Get out, now!" I pointed toward the door. I was done being cordial.

They looked at each other and huffed out the door.

It wasn't until my shift was over that things got worse. I'd finally calmed down enough to close out the bar. When walking to my car, I noticed right away that it had been vandalized. The windows were smashed out on the driver's side and my lights had also been shattered. I pulled out my cell phone and called the police, before heading back into the bar to wait for their arrival.

While I sat there, I was fuming. Gavin was to blame for all of this. He'd done this to my life. I dialed his number, not knowing what was going to come out of my mouth.

Vessa? You alright?

Funny that you care so much now.

Seriously, it's almost midnight. Where are you?

I'd be on my way home if your little whore hadn't of vandalized my car.

What are you talking about?

Your little girlfriend... you know, the one that is carrying your child?

The line went silent.

Gavin, you did this to yourself. Now you expect her to get an abortion? What kind of sick asshole are you? You have kids. You can't just force her to get an abortion because you screwed up. It's your responsibility to take care of that child.

I just want you, Ves.

That ship has sailed. There is no us and there never will be. You ruined everything and I can't stand to look at you.

Please give me another chance.

Hell to the no! Once the officers take my statement, I am coming home. I'm packing up the rest of my things and starting a new life. When we are separated for twelve months, I will file for divorce. Do you understand what I'm saying, Gavin? We are done!

Where are you going to go?

None of your damn business!

Please don't take away my kids, Ves.

I won't keep the kids from you, but you have no right to know where I'm going. This is my goodbye, Gavin. I gave you so many years of faithfulness and you just tossed me to the side. You have broken my heart more times than I care to count. I hope one day you can change and be the man that I always wanted you to be.

I hung up the phone right when I heard the car pulling into the parking lot. Two officers climbed out of the car and headed toward mine. "Damn, Vessa. Someone did a number on this." Tommy Barnes was someone that I'd known since grade school. I didn't know his partner at all.

"I don't know their names, but one of the girls that did this is carrying Gavin's child." I said it to get a rouse out of Tommy. He'd never really understood my dating Gavin.

"Are you kidding me right now?"

"Wish I was."

"I didn't know you were separated." He started walking around the car to assess the damage.

"I just found out."

"I knew you would find out. I wanted to tell you myself, but it wasn't my place." He wouldn't look at me after that comment.

"What do you mean? You knew?"

He leaned against the car and shook his head. "Vessa, I don't want to add fuel to the fire, but Gavin has been hooking up with random girls since high school. I never could understand how you could overlook something like that."

"Overlook? I had no idea! You knew this whole time?"

"The whole town knows, Vessa. He didn't really sneak around. Hell, I saw him last week holding hands with some young girl."

I ran toward the dumpster and puked. Apparently, I was the laughing stock of the whole damn town. This had been happening right in front of me for years. I couldn't face these people. I couldn't look at anyone the same. Not after they had all kept this dirty secret from me.

I pulled my keys out of my pocket and pushed Tommy to the side. "We're done here!"

"Vessa, wait! Don't do something you're going to regret." He knew me too well.

I didn't respond as I pulled away from both officers. I was fully aware that I was sitting on a mound of tempered glass and that it was pretty cold outside, especially with no window. All I cared about was killing that son of a bitch.

Gavin was sitting outside as I pulled into the driveway. He had a cigarette in his hand and stood up as I jumped out. I walked by him, ignoring that he even existed. Room by room, I packed up what we needed. I grabbed the kids out of their beds and walked them out to Gavin's car. Ever since he'd sat them down and gave them a version of what he'd done, they'd wanted nothing to do with him. Our youngest didn't quite understand, but he got that my heart was broken and that was enough for him.

The last thing I grabbed was a handgun. I planned to blow off his dick as I rode away.

He followed behind me. "What are you doing with that?"

I aimed it at his crotch.

"Vessa!"

I took the gun and shot out one of the tires on my vandalized car. The power of having the gun in my hand made me feel like I had the upper hand. I aimed it at our front door. "This is what you did to my heart." I fired once again, blowing out the glass.

Gavin put his hands in his hair, probably wondering if he was next. I knew the kids were in the car and I didn't have the balls to murder or shoot a man, especially someone they loved. I took the gun and smacked him in the jaw with it. He grabbed the gun from my hand and tossed it behind us on the ground. He had ahold of my arms and tried to pull me into his chest.

It took all of my might, but I freed myself from his hold. Then I punched him several times. "I hate you! I fucking hate you!"

"Vessa, I ended it. Were you really going to shoot me? You think I'm going to let you leave me in my own car? I'm calling the cops!"

"You have pretty much banged the whole town behind my back. Did you think I wouldn't find out? This car is in my name. Since your little whore ruined mine, I am taking this one. Call whoever you want. I will be long gone." I hated this man so much.

He put his head down and wouldn't answer.

"Goodbye, Gavin!"

I didn't wait for him to reply.

My kids were crying in the backseat so when I got a couple blocks away, I pulled over the car. "Everything is going to be okay, I promise."

I had no plan. The only relative that I had was an aunt that lived in West Virginia. It was a two-hour drive and I couldn't just show up on her doorstep. Luckily she owned a bar, so calling her this late wasn't going to be too damaging. I felt horrible since I didn't really keep in touch with her. She looked so much like my mother and the reminder was still painful for me.

Her raspy voice answered. *Hello?*

Aunt Sue, it's Vessa.

Vessa, honey, are you in trouble?

Finally, I started to cry. I couldn't believe that this was happening to me. *I'm in trouble and I don't have anywhere else to go.*

You come right here. Whatever it is, I am here for you, sweetie. You just get yourself here in one piece.

Can we come tonight?

The door will be open.

Thank you so much, Aunt Sue.

You are family. I don't turn my back on that. It's going to be alright, Vessa.

The kids and I cried the whole way, until they finally fell asleep. I assured them that we were going to start a new life and that I would make sure they still got to see their daddy. It would be rough, but I couldn't keep the kids from him. Sure, he'd call the cops and I would have trouble to deal with, but I needed to be away from him. This was my only option.

I was about twenty minutes from my aunt's place when the tractor-trailer came into view. The damn thing was on its side and sliding right for my car. I couldn't slam on my brakes and risk flipping the car with my kids in the back, so I swerved to avoid a head-on collision.

I woke up in a hospital room, with a police officer sitting beside me. He told me that my kids were with my aunt and then he hauled ass out of there, like I had the plague.

The next thing I knew, nurses and doctors were coming into the room to check my vitals. I needed to know if I was in some kind of trouble. If my children were okay, why was there a cop sitting next to me?

Chapter 5

Ramsey

By the time I got home, it was nearing five in the morning. I was exhausted, but couldn't seem to relax enough to get a couple more hours of sleep in. That mother's face looking over at me was haunting me. Don't get me wrong, I was glad she was going to be okay. The last thing I wanted was another mother dying too soon on my watch.

For the next few weeks, I avoided the bar and Sue's phone calls. I didn't want to be involved in the accident anymore and I was sure that she was calling to talk to me about why else I hadn't been by. After exhausting all of the excuses that I could conjure up, I finally had to take her call.

Hello.

Ramsey Towers, why haven't you answered my messages?

Sorry, Sue. I've been busy.

Doing what? Lots of cats stuck up in trees?

Is there something that I can do for you?

You're damn right there is. My niece and her children would like to thank you for what you did for them. I'm making you dinner and you ain't telling me you can't come. I know you don't have plans, so don't even think about using that as an excuse. Be at my house at six.

Sue... I...

Six sharp.

The woman hung up before I could argue with her. I hated to be put into a position like this to begin with, but being forced to socialize was even worse. They were going to ask questions and I just didn't want to have to answer any.

The rest of my afternoon consisted of a six pack of beer and a million excuses of how I could get out of going over to Sue's place. By the time that six o'clock came around, I was out of beer and ideas, so I showered and headed over.

I'd no sooner pulled up outside when a little boy came running toward me. "How come you didn't use your siren when you came here?"

I chuckled, considering how he thought that police vehicles had to have the siren on at all times. "There wasn't an emergency."

"My name is Logan. My birthday is in two weeks and I am going to be six." When he smiled, I noticed that he was missing a couple teeth.

"Nice to meet you, Logan." I started to walk past the boy.

"What's your name?"

This kid wasn't going to let me out of his sight until he was done grilling me. "My name is Ramsey."

"What kind of name is that? It sounds like a good name for a dog." He had his hands on his hips, waiting for me to reply.

"It was my grandfather's name."

"Why?"

Suddenly, a voice cut in to our conversation. His sister, who was a lot taller, came walking toward us. "Don't pay attention to my brother. He never shuts up."

"You shut up, Asha! You're a butthead!"

"I'm telling Mom!" She ran back inside and I could hear her calling out for her mother.

The little guy followed her into the house, so I followed behind him. Sue came walking out of the back of the house with a kitchen towel wrapped around her hand. I could see the red coming through the fabric. "You're just in time for the entertainment. I seem to have cut my hand pretty bad."

I'd never been in her house before, but I followed the woman back to a bathroom, where she started running her hand under the faucet. "How'd you do this?"

"Cutting a damn onion. Do you believe that? I've been cutting up onions my whole life and when I finally have company over, I manage to cut off half a finger."

I reached up into the cabinet and helped Sue get her wound clean. While helping her apply a bandage, I heard someone walking up behind us. "How bad is it?"

I turned around to see a very different woman than I had seen lying in that hospital bed. After just a short time, her bruises were almost gone. Even where she'd had stitches had healed up nicely. The woman wore little makeup, but what she did have on accented the coolest-looking hazel eyes.

When she kept waiting for me to say something, I realized that I had been staring. "Sorry... I think she's going to be fine. It may be best if one of us does the rest of the cutting."

She smiled and then turned her attention back to her aunt. "You sure you don't need stitches?"

"I have survived worse. Let's just get dinner done and not worry about me."

I moved out of Sue's way so she could lead us toward the kitchen. She grabbed a pack of cigarettes and walked toward a sliding glass door. "Everything is ready except for the lasagna. It has about twenty more minutes to go. I'll be back in when I'm done with this." She held up her cigarette as she walked out the door.

I placed my hands on the countertop, trying to avoid making eye contact with the woman. She cleared her throat, forcing me to do it anyway. "Cat got your tongue?"

She was an attractive woman and I think she knew it. Her long blonde hair was perfectly straightened and it hung down her back. She was wearing an old Van Halen t-shirt that accented her breasts. One of her arms was full of tattoos, while her other arm only had ink on the wrist.

Noticing that I was pretty much staring at her chest, I looked up and creased my brows. "I'm not much for conversation."

"How come? Aren't you the sheriff? Surely you have to interact with people." She was putting the plates out on the table as she spoke.

"I do my job and mind my business."

"Alrighty then." She turned her back to me and mumbled something.

A long time ago, I would have challenged her attitude. That was the old me. The new me didn't care what she thought. I just wanted the night to be over with. "Are you feeling better?"

"My head still hurts, but I'm under a lot of stress, so it may not even be from the accident."

I wasn't going to ask her business. By asking hers, I would have to explain mine and that was never going to happen.

"I left my old life, if you're wondering. The kids and me, well, we will survive."

I didn't mean to smile, but she had this spunky attitude that was both intriguing to me and also a warning sign that I need to steer clear. I hated that the kids had to be involved in something as major as picking up and leaving. Did they have a father out there somewhere missing them? "Sorry to hear that."

"Yeah, I bet you are. I just wanted you to know, in case you had any ideas about us hooking up. I'm not interested and it would just be a waste of your time. I know my aunt thinks that you and I could be good friends, but I don't expect anything from you."

"I didn't come here for that. I can assure you that I have no intentions when it comes to you or anyone else. I don't date and I don't have friends." I sounded like a serial killer.

"Then we are on the same page. Good. Now we can enjoy our dinner." She held her hand out and waited for me to shake it. "My name is Vessa. I'm a recently separated mother of two. I don't have a pot to piss in, so I moved in with my aunt. That's my story."

I shook her hand, knowing damn well that she expected me to respond the same way to her. "I'm Ramsey Towers. It's nice to meet you."

"Mr. Secretive? You aren't going to divulge any information about yourself?" This was a bad idea.

"I have no story to tell. I'm the sheriff of the next town over. I do my job and mind my own business."

She backed away from me and shook her head. "Clearly, you don't want to talk about it. I know when to back off. Listen, I just wanted to say thank you for taking care of my kids the night of the accident and sitting with me at the hospital. It was nice not to wake up all alone."

"Just doing my job."

Sue came walking in at the perfect time. I was about to run out of reasons why I didn't want to talk about my past.

For dinner, we all sat at a large dining room table. The little guy, Logan, sat across from me, staring a hole into me. "Have you ever shot someone?"

"Logan!" His mother didn't like the question much.

Knowing his age, I chuckled and sat down my fork for a second. "Being a police officer isn't about shooting people. I do a lot of other things for the people of my town."

"Like what?" He wasn't going to give up.

"Well, you saw me tend to your car accident. I also investigate when crimes have been committed and try to stop the bad guys before anything else happens."

"Like having to shoot 'em?"

"Logan, I am not going to say it again!"

"Exactly like that."

"When I grow up, I am going to be a superhero. Mom says that cops just write tickets and act like jerks. I don't want to be a jerk."

It was hard not to laugh, but as I looked over and saw Vessa's face turning a bright shade of red, I couldn't help it. I'd been called worse and it didn't make me want to change occupations.

The girl, Asha, asked to be excused. She had blonde hair like her mother and I could see the resemblance in them. She seemed polite at the dinner table, but once she and her brother were excused, I could hear them going at it in the living room. Finally, their mother had to get up and intervene.

I helped Sue clean up the table, while Vessa stayed with the kids. It was better that way, since I didn't want to have to talk to her. Everyone wanted to know my story. I was just sick of it. Couldn't people mind their business and live their own lives?

"Did you enjoy the food?" Sue asked as I handed her a plate.

"You know I love everything you make. Hell, I'd be skin and bones if it weren't for your cooking." Jules had always done the cooking in our marriage. I honestly never learned how.

"My niece is a good girl. We all got problems, but she's got a big heart."

"Are you trying to set me up? You know I'm a private man. I'd be no good for her or anyone else." It was true. I'd given up on love.

"I think that you could be friends. You two are the same. Always dwelling on the past. I don't know your story, Ramsey, but I know something's made you be the person that you are now. Whatever it is, you can't hold it in. It's not healthy. I ain't saying you have to date her, but there is nothing wrong with being friends with someone. Besides, she's taking over at the bar and you are going to have to get used to seeing her."

"When is that happening?" I was going to miss the way Sue never asked questions.

"When she's feeling up to it."

Vessa came walking in, which put an end to the uncomfortable conversation. "Are you going to stick around for a while? I can make coffee."

I waved my hand around. "No thanks. I need to get going. Thanks for dinner, though."

The women walked me out to the porch and said their goodbyes. All in all, it wasn't such a bad time. They didn't press me about things and I appreciated that. Maybe one day I would be able to open up and socialize again the way I used to. I just missed my girls too much to be able to let them go.

Chapter 6

Vessa

The accident set me back, but gave me time to help the kids get adjusted to living in a new place. I was happy to see how easily they were able to make new friends. My recovery was slow and I didn't want to chance reinjuring myself, especially my head.

Since my aunt was so happy that we were there, she'd pretty much made up her mind that I was going to slowly start taking over her shifts at her bar. Her late husband had left it to her, and since his death she'd devoted every second to keeping it up and running.

It needed some TLC, but it had character. My aunt Sue had collected a bunch of unique decor through the years. Since her main business was travelers, mainly truckers, you can imagine that some of the items were vulgar. Several sets of plastic breasts were hung on the walls with beads hanging over them, like Mardi Gras. It was my son who noticed them all, the moment he first stepped foot in the place. I think my aunt was devastated over it. She wasn't used to kids, but was trying her hardest to get to know both of them.

Some days it was hard because she reminded me so much of my mother, who I missed terribly. In other ways, it was a godsend that she was here, opening her home and life to us. I appreciated her so much for it.

When I got out of the hospital, Gavin begged me to come home. He made all of his usual promises about changing, but it was all bullshit. His girlfriend was pregnant and during one of my heated arguments with my mother-in-law, she'd slipped and admitted that the girl was living at my house. To think about her being there and sleeping in my bed made me sick.

The longer I was away from Gavin, the more I realized that it was exactly what I should have done. His lying was continuous and I didn't deserve that—neither did my kids. To keep the peace though, we agreed to meet halfway every other weekend, so that he could have them for a couple days.

After the first visit, the kids didn't seem too thrilled about their father's new relationship. I'd asked him to hold off on telling them, but apparently the girl had no place to go. Gavin told me that her parents had kicked her out when they found out she'd dropped out of school to hang out at a tattoo parlor and get knocked up.

My daughter seemed more upset than my son. I think it was because she was old enough to understand why I'd left their dad. She cried that night, once we got home and she was tucked in bed. In order to cheer her up, my aunt went to the paint store while she was at school and we painted her room her favorite color—making it really her room.

Since I was one of my aunt's only living relatives, and the closest, she'd always told me that I was like a daughter to her. I regretted being so distant to her for so long, especially when I knew she didn't have anyone else. I think some days she overexerted herself trying to make us feel welcome.

Some days were better than others. I could put on a fake smile and pretend that my life was right where I wanted it to be, but inside was a different story. I was literally dying inside. To be cheated on, repeatedly, was awful. I felt like it was all my fault. Most nights I would cry myself to sleep, or not sleep at all. With Gavin continually calling me, it made it even worse to wear that smile. I did my best around the kids, knowing that my happiness fed theirs.

For the most part, my day-to-day struggles to accept my new life were increasingly improving. I didn't have the money or resources to seek professional counseling, but knowing that my aunt was around did help. Going back to work helped even more.

After that sheriff came for dinner, and had been so quiet, I couldn't believe that he would be one to hang out in a bar. It wasn't that he was mean. He was just not sociable.

But there he was... walking in the door with that same hard look on his face. I have no idea why I did it, but I ducked in the back room to avoid him seeing me. Frantically, I started straightening my clothes and looking at my reflection in the metal door to see if I looked decent.

I'd never cared what any of my patrons thought of me. I was always that married bartender that was a good listener and nothing else. It wasn't like I was desperately trying to impress anyone. This was just all so new to me. Still, ever since I woke up in that hospital and saw him sitting there, a part of me had to know more about him.

I was never the kind of girl to hit on a man, or even one that was remotely promiscuous. I'd loved Gavin for as long as I could remember, but here was this hot man that was so mysterious. I couldn't help wanting to impress him from afar. He would never get into my pants—I was hardly interested in hooking up. Most men were pigs anyway, or so I'd come to notice. This one probably had an affair and lost everything when he had to pay out of his ass for alimony. I'd heard pretty much every story.

While trying to make excuses for my sudden vanity, the back room door flew open, slamming into me.

"Sue, you got customers out... Holy shit, miss, I am so sorry."

I held onto my jaw and backed myself up against the wall. The pain was instant, but the embarrassment took a few seconds. That hot ass sheriff had his eyes on mine and his hand on my arm.

I pulled away and started walking past him, out to the bar area. After looking around and noticing nobody else, I turned around to see him standing there. I moved my jaw around, realizing that the pain was already starting to subside. My cheek would be red, I was sure.

"My aunt isn't here." I grabbed a glass out of the freezer and put it against my injured face.

"I can see that." He put his hand up to assess my face, but dropped it back down just as quick. "I'm real sorry that happened. I thought you were your aunt and I usually say hi to her. When I don't, she gets all mad at me. Are you alright?"

His voice was deep and raspy. I bet he could sing in a real sexy voice. Making it a point to not look him directly in the eye, I answered him. "I'll be fine. Obviously, I am no virgin to injury."

Did I really just say that? What had come over me?

"Yeah, I've noticed."

I didn't give him another second to laugh about my predicament. "So, what can I get you?"

"What's on the menu tonight?"

"Meatloaf with mashed potatoes and stewed tomatoes." My aunt had made them up and baked them at home before I came into work. It was easier to just reheat them as they were ordered. She'd said that the truckers loved her home-cooked food.

"Sounds great. I'll have that and a Jack and Coke. No ice!"

He obviously knew what he wanted. I started making his drink without replying. This was the second time that I had seen him in normal clothes and not his usual attire, which consisted of an all-black uniform with a black baseball cap that had a police emblem on it. Tonight he was wearing jeans and a t-shirt that revealed every muscle on his upper body.

Yeah, he had to be a cheater. There was no way that this man could ever have just one woman, with the way he looked. His hair was in between a brown and dark blonde, but his facial hair was darker. I could tell from the five o'clock shadow that was starting to appear. Perhaps he hadn't shaved this morning at all.

I continued to glance at him as I handed him the glass. "Do you eat behind the bar, or are you going to sit down somewhere?"

It was a good question but as he cocked his brow at me, I realized that the way it came out was quite bitchy.

Without saying a single word, he grabbed his glass and walked away.

My customer service skills were falling short. I thought about apologizing, but he didn't seem like he would care either way, so I headed to the back to make his food. When I came back out, I found him sitting at a table in the far corner. It was the darkest, most remote table in the whole place. I sat his plate on the table and went to walk away when I felt him grab my arm again. "You think I could have some silverware?"

I looked down at the table and realized that he didn't have anything to eat his food with. "Oops! Be right back."

Once I got behind the bar, I whispered profanities at myself for being so air-headed. Ramsey was sitting back in his seat with a smirk on his face. "Here you go. Sorry about that."

"So are you new at this?" I took offense to his question.

"No! I have been bartending for a long time. I'm just out of practice, I guess." I watched him start cutting his meat with his fork. "Do you need anything else?"

"Nope, you can get back to whatever you were doing and pretend that I'm not even here. If I need anything, I will holler."

He was cold again and I didn't like it. Maybe he was offended by my tattoos, like some people were. They only showed on my one arm. My clothes hid the other few and I was dressed appropriately, but I knew I wasn't ugly otherwise. This was just weird to me. For so long, my looks had gotten me good tips and lots of conversation. I wasn't attention hungry, but I didn't like to be brushed off.

A few scruffy-looking men came walking in the bar. I turned my focus on them and ignored Ramsey like he'd requested. When the men had their drinks and had ordered food, they headed toward the billiards area. I prepared their food and headed out to deliver it to them. The first thing I noticed was the one guy staring at my tits as I reached over to put his plate on the table. "What happened to the old lady?"

"She's my aunt. She doesn't work nights anymore."

"Her loss was our gain." The other guy said while nudging his buddy. "You're a real pretty one. You got a man somewhere?"

I'd been asked this a million times before, except then, I really did have a man. "Sorry guys, I have a girlfriend."

Did I actually just claim to be a lesbian to avoid these guys?

Oh yes, I really did. To make matters worse, I said it loud enough that even Ramsey heard it. I saw him shake his head before finishing off his drink. I knew there were amazing parents out there that were homosexual, and had nothing against them, but it upset me right away that I had lied about myself like that. Still, in my line of work, it was worth it.

The bar filled up shortly after that and soon I was too busy to care about what I should or shouldn't have said in front of the sheriff. I still don't understand why I even cared about his opinion anyway. I had too much on my plate to worry about. Ramsey came up to the bar and I quickly gave him a refill. He didn't smile or even say thanks, so I was feeling like he had major issues in his life and maybe he was just a mean person. It was a shame, because he really was a nice-looking man. Had his attitude been better, he could probably have any woman he wanted.

My eyes followed him walking toward the pool tables. After a brief couple of words to the two men, he was grabbing a stick and starting a match. I missed shooting pool and socializing with all of my old customers. Here, I was just a new face. It would wear off and I would be stuck tending to overly horny truck drivers and an asshole sheriff from the town over. It didn't sound very appealing at all.

The sounds of the balls breaking were louder than the jukebox and I couldn't help but look over every time I heard it. The familiar sound kept my attention and I found myself staring at the men playing.

I gasped when I watched Ramsey bend down and stroke the stick before cutting a ball in the side pocket. He clenched his jaw when he concentrated. It was extremely sexy. Every muscle in his arm moved when he held the stick. He didn't see me looking and I was glad. Maybe it was because I had not had sex in so long, but watching him gave me chills up my spine.

When I noticed that his drink was getting low, I scurried over and sat a new one where he was sitting. He looked down at the glass and then up to me. "I have legs. If I need something, I'll let you know."

I wanted to kick him in the balls. I was just trying to be nice and he was being a complete dick. What was with me being attracted to assholes?

I pouted behind the bar, only looking into the room when necessary. By the time midnight came around, the bar emptied and only the three men remained. I could tell that they'd all had too much to drink. Their voices were loud and they were rambling on and on to each other.

Finally, the two truckers pulled out money and handed it to Ramsey. I couldn't believe the 'good sheriff' was gambling. If he was nicer, I would have teased him about it. Honestly, I wanted him to just walk out and leave. Instead, he headed right for the bar. Without saying anything, he pulled out thirty bucks and slid it across the bar. Then he adjusted his hat and walked out the door.

I shook my head and started cleaning up so that I could close and go home.

Nearly thirty minutes later, I was locking the door and heading out to my aunt's car. I rummaged through my oversized purse to locate car keys. When I had them in my hand, I dropped them on the ground, by accident. Laughing caught me off guard, coming from behind me. This was just a little town. There was barely any kind of crime here, but I still felt scared.

When I turned around, I spotted one of the truck drivers. He was fast approaching me. "It's a shame you only like pussy. I could give you a real good time, if you'd let me."

I backed myself up against my car. "I bet. Did you need something?" My teeth were chattering. I was so scared.

He got closer and brushed my blonde hair away from my face. "Maybe you just need a good fuck to turn you back straight."

I ducked my body and moved away from him. He smelled of beer and motor oil and I wanted nothing to do with the situation. "No thanks. Maybe you should just head out."

He grabbed me by both of my arms. "Why don't you come back to my truck with me? I got a big bed in the back with plenty of room for both of us."

As I struggled to free my arms, the man's arms were jerked off me. When he fell to the ground, I looked up and saw Ramsey standing between us. "You alright?" He looked right at me.

I hugged myself and backed up against the car, without answering him. I'd just been assaulted and I wasn't sure how I was feeling.

Ramsey grabbed the guy by his shirt and pushed him towards his truck, and away from me. "Get your ass out of here, before I put you behind bars for the night!"

His threat worked and the guy hauled ass to his truck. Ramsey waited until he pulled out of the parking lot before turning around to me. "Miss, you alright?"

"It's Vessa. My name is Vessa."

"Are you alright?" He reached for my arm, but I pulled away.

"I'm just peachy."

"We'll then, get in your car and go home. Those guys were talking all night about what they wanted to do to you. I parked around back and waited to make sure it didn't happen. You need to be more careful."

"I'm glad you were here."

He clenched his jaw again. "Just try to be more careful, miss."

When he started to walk away, it irked me that he kept calling me that. "It's Vessa!"

He never turned around and acknowledged me or my name. Instead, he climbed in his truck and waited for me to pull out of the parking lot before he did the same.

That man was annoying and an ass. I was more certain of that then before.

Chapter 7

Ramsey

Trouble.

That is what she was to me.

A real pain in my ass.

Ever since Sue had filled me in on letting her niece take over her shifts, I had avoided the bar like the plague. There was just something about her that I was drawn to and I didn't like it.

After nearly taking off her face with the door, I stayed far away, keeping our conversations to a minimum. I wasn't ready to open up and, clearly, she had her own skeletons in her closet. Who else travels in the middle of the night with two kids? There was definitely something going on with her.

I think it made things easier after she announced that she wasn't interested in men. Of course, it made me wonder if that was just a ploy to get those guys off her back. I knew the one was going to be a problem. The whole time we were shooting our matches, they were deciding which one of them was going to get his turn first with her.

I wasn't new to that game. Most of those guys went weeks without seeing their wives. They were horny and willing to do anything for a piece of ass. Vessa wasn't like the women that usually ran these types of establishments. She was beautiful and had curves in all the right places. Hell, even her hairstyle was too nice for this rundown place. They'd probably mistaken her for some ex-stripper, the way she was all done up for work.

I was suspicious of her prior occupation until she told me that she was a bartender. Obviously, the place she worked at last had a different kind of clientele. This bar was rundown and housed only the dirtiest of people. I picked it because of that. It was the kind of place where nobody wanted to know who you were; where nobody would ask questions about my life and my past.

Though haunted by their memory, the next couple months went by quickly. I only went to the bar a couple nights a week, never giving Vessa a moment to ask me questions. I could tell that it offended her. The more distant and cold I acted, the more she seemed to be interested. Some may have thought it to be funny, but I wasn't one of them.

I was used to my life. It was fine with me to go home and never communicate with anyone outside of work. Shooting pool was my only escape and even then, I never had to talk about my life. When people shot for money, they didn't really ask your whole life story.

Each time I went into the bar for a hot meal, she was there, with those sexy eyes, trying to figure me out. I didn't blame her. It was what a good bartender did. It was what a cop did.

I often wondered if she'd asked Sue about me, and if she had, what was said about it. Nobody knew the real truth. None of them knew that I carried the burden of killing them. They didn't know that I was living in a real life Hell.

One night, after a long shift where someone was in a horrific car accident, I found myself walking into the bar. My guard was down and I was wearing my guilt on my shoulders. Vessa was at the bar, talking to someone I recognized as a regular. She glanced over at me and smiled. Regrettably, I smiled back at her. Knowing that this was the first real time that I had showed any type of emotion, aside from being in a bad mood, she put herself out there. "How are you today, Sheriff?"

"Do you really want to know?" I sat down on a stool across from her and watched as she made my usual drink and slid it over.

"It's my job to ask."

"That isn't what I asked you." I realized that this was the most that I'd talked to her, aside from the times where a catastrophe had occurred.

She let out a giggle and shook her head. "Do you really want to know my opinion? I mean, you hardly say two words to me each time you come in to eat. I can take a hint and I know when my company isn't wanted. Just let me know what you want to eat and I will get it for you so you can head over to your corner and eat in private." She seemed offended immediately and turned around so that I couldn't see her face.

The person at the other end of the bar paid their tab and left, which meant it was only Vessa and me in the bar. We were in between the early and late dinner rush. This was a situation that I didn't want to be in. "It ain't about you, Vessa." I sort of yelled it across the bar. I don't know why I cared about her feelings, but I needed her to know that.

She walked back in front of me and put her hands on the bar to lean forward. "You actually know my name now?"

"I've always known your name. Look, I'm not the kind of guy that you want to know." She needed to stay away from me. I was bad luck and she was trying to start over.

"I will be the judge of who I keep company with, you got that?" She kept leaning in, waiting for me to respond. "You have no idea what I've been through. Don't you dare judge me."

I liked that she held her ground. Most people steered clear, but she kept pressing—waiting for an opening like the one I had just given her. "I stand corrected. I don't socialize."

"I see you socialize every time you play pool. Don't tell me you aren't capable."

I shook my head and regretted walking through the door. "That's different."

She walked away from me. I watched her leave the bar area and head over to the pool table. She picked up the cue ball and turned to face me. "Since we have to be around each other, I think it is only fair that I get to know you, at least a little."

I grabbed my glass and headed in her direction.

This was a terrible idea.

I approached her and looked down at the petite woman. "Only the winner gets to ask questions." This would guarantee that I didn't have to tell her anything about myself.

She smiled, while walking toward the bar again. Without looking back, she called out, "I'm not that good."

I was going to be alright. I would beat her ass a couple of times and she would give up on the questioning. "Just try your best. We can play nine ball and you don't have to call your shot."

She grabbed a pool stick and fumbled it between her fingers, like she'd never held one before. "Is this right?"

I nodded and decided to give her the break. She positioned the cue ball and did her best to break up the rack. A few balls moved, but they didn't go far. I took my time, running out the balls, never giving her another shot. "I guess I get to ask the first question."

She seemed defeated, but this was her idea.

Vessa held her hands up. "Okay, be gentle."

"What are you running from?"

Her face got red and I could tell she was affected by my question. "I'm not running. I needed a new start after a bad relationship." She bent down and racked the balls again.

"We don't have to play this game if you don't want to."

Without a second thought, she stood up. "No, I'm getting the hang of it."

I shook my head as I broke up the rack. They scattered all over the table before two went into pockets. She leaned against the wall, watching me run out four more balls. I missed the fifth shot by nearly a quarter inch. Vessa walked toward the table and bent down to take her shot. She made a ball and jumped up and down. I couldn't help but notice her supple tits bouncing up and down. I was a man; a man who hadn't been with a woman in a very long time. With her next shot lined up, she leaned down and shot, but missed.

I looked over to see her pouting as I ran out the last few balls. Unlike the first game, I didn't wait for her to even start racking before asking the next question. "What's it like being a lesbian? Is it hard raising kids?"

She immediately broke out into laughter. "I wouldn't know. You'll have to ask a lesbian. Way to waste a question, though."

I knew it. I knew she was telling those guys a lie. "I just assumed... I mean, you did tell those men."

"Yeah, I did. I wouldn't give them the time of day. As far as I'm concerned, all men are scum of the earth. No offense or anything. I just have a certain opinion about the male race."

"No offense taken. You can only judge what you know."

"Yeah, well my husband did a number on me. I've sworn off men, but not switched teams, at least not yet."

Just as I bent down to take another shot, three people walked into the bar. Vessa hung up her stick and headed to tend to them. I waited a little while, thinking the crowd would eat and leave, but more people came in. After having another few drinks and eating a sandwich, that I didn't even have to order, I called it a night. I tried to at least say goodbye to Vessa, but she was too busy to notice.

While driving home, I realized that it was the first time I'd almost opened up. I wasn't real sure how I felt about that. Sure, I knew the girl had no chance of beating me, so I wasn't that worried about it. Still, for some reason, it seemed like I might want to talk to her again. It made sense since I saw her at least two to three times a week.

I finished off the rest of my bottle of Jack at home. The more I drank, the more I pictured Vessa bending over taking shots. It was wrong, but it had been so long and I had needs, even if I lived a solitary life. I didn't know how monks did it, honestly.

The next morning I regretted opening up to Vessa. She was going to expect things to progress until she got her turn to ask questions. I needed to find another place to eat, or figure out how to work my stove and cook for myself. Ramen noodles weren't going to suffice seven nights a week. Knowing Sue, if she got wind of me not coming in, she'd probably hunt my ass down. It was time for me decide one way or another how I wanted to live the rest of my life. Did I really want to be alone with no friends?

Just as I was considering opening up and being more sociable, everything came crashing down on me when I got to police station. I'd no sooner got into my office, when my deputy came in and tossed the local paper on my desk. The front page made me feel ill.

TOWN SHERIFF LOST FAMILY IN CAR CRASH

"Sir, did you know they was goin' to print this?"

I was so enraged that someone had dug into my private life and announced it to the whole town. I grabbed my jacket and started walking back out. "If you need me, you can reach me on my cell."

I headed straight to the little town paper and waited for them to open for the day. While flinging the wad of newspaper on the editor's desk, I tried my best to keep myself calm. "What the hell is this? Who would print this?"

"Sheriff, it wasn't me, but you have to understand that this is public information. The people of the town want to know you."

I leaned over the desk. "My life is none of their damn business!"

After arguing for another twenty minutes, I climbed in my truck and headed straight for the liquor store. Everyone now knew what I was running from. I couldn't hide from it any longer. I would be judged, consoled, and harassed about my feelings. Never again could I just live out my days in peace. I wanted to just pack my shit up and leave, if I had to face one single person about my girls.

I wasn't ready to talk about them; to tell people how I'd taken their lives.

Since the little town paper was usually a freebie to only the town people, I managed to grab as many copies off lawns as I could. Then I went into the gas station and the grocery store and removed them as well. Sure, the news would travel, but it was still early and I was sure that I had removed at least half of what was out there.

To free some of the stress that was overwhelming me, I bought two bottles of Jack before heading back to the cabin. I needed to be alone. I wanted to disappear.

Chapter 8

Vessa

Did I feel bad for making Ramsey think I couldn't play pool?

Not really!

He was hiding something, and even though it was none of my business, I was more intrigued than ever to find out what had made him the way he was.

We still hadn't had a real conversation, but I felt like progress was being made. Maybe I was one of those people who thought they could fix people. Obviously I wasn't, since my own life had gone to shit. Ramsey was just one of those people that you were dying to know what broke them.

Since he had been in the night before, I never expected him to stumble into the bar the very next day. I'd only been there for about thirty minutes when I heard the door open and shut. During the day, it was pretty quiet without the jukebox running.

Right away, I could tell that he'd already been drinking. He barely made it to the edge of the bar before struggling to climb up on a stool. I dropped the rag that I had in my hand and approached him. "What brings you in here this time of day, Sheriff?" He was still in his uniform, which I might add, made him look even sexier than usual.

This is what drove me crazy the most. I never had met a man that I couldn't stop looking at. Honestly, I'd never been interested in anyone except Gavin. Technically,

I was still married by law, but in my heart I knew my marriage was over.

"Does it matter? Give me a drink and mind your business, for once!" As the slurred words came out of his mouth, I backed away from where he sat. I could smell the liquor and I knew when it was time for someone to be cut off. Based on the size of Ramsey and how much I had seen him drink before, I knew that this was far from what I had ever seen.

I poured him a glass of coke and pretended to put Jack in it. When I handed it to him, our hands touched and he kept his over mine for a second.

Was it a plea for help?

This man was so hard to read.

"I'll just be over there if you need me." I wasn't about to argue with someone who was this drunk. Clearly, he shouldn't be out driving, so the best way to keep him safe was to appease him and keep feeding him soda until he sobered up and realized what a fool he had been for driving in the first place.

Ramsey was quiet for about a half hour and then out of nowhere, he stood up and started yelling. "You wouldn't understand! Nobody can! Do you hear me? Nobody could ever understand!" He was pointing at me, but backing up as he tried to stand still.

I'd seen many drunk people and even had to call the cops a few times when things got out of hand, but clearly Ramsey was battling demons and I wasn't about to be the person who got him fired for drinking on the job. I held up my hands in the air. "You're right! I don't understand. Just sit back down and we don't have to talk about it."

He shook his head and mumbled something before approaching the stool to sit back down. Unfortunately, he missed it and tumbled to the ground. Instinct sent me running around to help him. He was way too heavy for me to lift, so I grabbed onto his arms and guided him to stand back up. He took his hands and grabbed both of my arms. "Jules?"

"Who is...?" He didn't give me time to ask.

"Baby, I am so sorry. It's all my fault. I miss you so much, baby. I miss our family. I can't do this anymore."

I had no idea who Jules was, but he was obviously thinking she was me, because he pulled me into his arms and held me there as he continued to talk. I stilled my body and closed my eyes, not sure of what to do next. I wasn't exactly scared of Ramsey, but since I knew nothing about him, I also knew that he could be a woman beater or maybe even worse. He didn't just smell of booze. No, there was some kind of woodsy smelling cologne that I'd smelled before on him. He pulled my body even closer, shoving my face into his hard chest. "I just need another chance, Jules. I want it all back. Please, baby, don't be dead. Say it was all a bad dream. Tell me it wasn't real!"

His words cut through my heart. He'd lost someone, possibly more than one person, to death. This poor man was more broken than I could have ever imagined. My hands wrapped around his waist before I even knew I was doing it. "It's going to be okay. You aren't alone."

I could feel real tears hitting the top of my head as he kissed it. As absurd as the situation was to me, it was very real for him. I didn't want to pretend to be someone that I wasn't, but I certainly didn't want to piss the big guy off. After a few minutes, I was able to pull away. I got him sitting on the floor and ran to call my aunt.

She told me to just lock up and drive Ramsey home. In the frantic situation I was in, I'd neglected to ask where the man lived. It was a feat getting him into his truck and finding his keys, which were actually left in the ignition, but driving around until he told me where to go was even worse.

Finally, as he leaned against the passenger window, he led me up a long dirt road. It was scary and seemed like I was driving to a place to be raped and killed where I'd never be discovered. I stuck to my gut feeling and continued on until I came to a cabin in a clearing.

Ramsey opened the passenger door and let me guide him into the house.

The place was a mess. Take-out food boxes were sitting all over the tables and the sink was filled with silverware and cups. Ramsey disappeared into a back room and I was hoping that he passed out, finally.

After I called my aunt and told her where to come, I hung up and looked around the cabin. The living and dining area had high ceilings that showed the original beams to the cabin, but a set of stairs with three doors above, told me there were other rooms.

I walked into the kitchen and looked around at the exposed wood logs on all the outside walls to the house. It gave it a country charm that I fell in love with. It wasn't hard to find where Ramsey kept the trash bags. I grabbed one from under the sink and tossed all of the trash that was laying around into it. Then I washed the dishes in the sink. While wiping down all of the tables, I heard a loud bang from the direction that Ramsey had gone.

I found him on the floor with his shirt half on and stuck over his head. Quietly, I kneeled down beside him and helped with the shirt. Right away, my eyes had to do a double take. The man was sculpted, I'd already known that, but he had beautiful tattoos on each of his upper arms. He began mumbling something I couldn't make out as I traced them with my fingers. The artwork was magnificent, but what really caught my eye was the name that was intricately place inside of the masterpiece.

I twisted my body to look at the matching tattoo on the other arm and noticed that there was only one difference in the mirror image. Another name was displayed.

My body began to tremble when I realized what I was looking at. The man had built two shrines for his loved ones. I didn't know how they died, but they were gone and he was lost.

As I focused on his painful reality, he caught me off guard and pulled me into him. When his lips found mine, I kept still. The Jack was prominent on his breath, and maybe I should have stopped him, but as he continued to place tender kisses over my lips, I found myself responding to them.

These kisses were so desperate and necessary for him. If I'd lost the one I loved tragically and thought that for just one moment I could touch them again, I'd be doing the same thing.

It wasn't just the way he was kissing me though. I felt something, even though this had nothing to do with me. His lips ignited a fire that I had never felt before. Maybe I was too caught up in the moment to realize what was actually happening, but I grabbed the back of his neck and kissed him back more.

Finally, as we both paused to catch our breath, I felt his head touch down on one of my shoulders. "I love you, Jules," he whispered.

It broke my heart again hearing him going through the motions of sharing a moment with his wife. This poor man had been holding all of his emotional despair inside. This wasn't healthy. He needed help; possibly someone that could provide advice on how he could move on with his life in a way where he would allow himself to smile again.

Shortly after his comment to his wife, he climbed into his bed, sort of like a child would, and passed out. I noticed the bed was made and that in the living room there was a pillow and blanket on the couch. He must not have liked sleeping in a bed without her.

As the pieces to the puzzle started to come together, I saw a different man before me. I didn't go through his things any more than I already had. It wasn't my place to know this story. It was going to be hard enough to face him when he woke up and realized what he'd done.

That kiss.

The kiss was a huge mistake on my part. He was never going to want to be friends with someone that had let that happen.

Still, I found it to be some kind of mission to help Ramsey as much as I could.

When I heard the horn outside, I stuck Ramsey's keys by the front door and saw myself out. Maybe since I had straightened up the place, he wouldn't be too hard on me. I doubted it though.

While reaching in the truck to grab my purse, I noticed a stack of newspaper in the backseat. It was the local tribune paper for the town that Ramsey was the sheriff of. The whole stack was the same issue and it was about Ramsey's family that had died.

I understood immediately why he was in the shape that he was in. This article had caused Ramsey to lose control. He had drank enough every night to make himself forget. I grabbed one of the papers, but left the rest the way they were. Before I climbed in the car with my aunt and kids, I stuck the article in my purse. This was Ramsey's story to share, not mine. It was apparent that he didn't want people knowing his business. I wanted to march right into that newspaper office and give them a piece of my mind.

I didn't know Ramsey, at all really, but what I'd learned today had explained pretty much everything. I knew for a fact that he hadn't given permission for this to get out. He wanted his secrets to stay that way. Everything would change for Ramsey with the town knowing the truth. His tough façade would be replaced with pity.

Once I climbed in the car with my family, I knew that he was going to be on my mind until I saw him again. It wasn't just his problems that I was concerned about. That kiss may not have been meant for me, but it sure did a number on me, just the same.

Chapter 9

Ramsey

I woke up and had no idea where I was. After assessing my surroundings, I realized that I was in my bedroom at the cabin. It was dark outside and I could hear the crickets and other insects outside making their normal nightly sounds.

As I tried to stand up, my headache kicked in, sending me back down on the bed.

The weirdest thing was that when I went out into the living room, it was cleaner. A trash bag was tied and leaning against the kitchen entryway. I looked further and saw that even the dishes were done. Thinking that someone had been in my house, I headed toward the door and found that it was not only locked, but my keys were right where I usually left them.

Had I been that inebriated that I didn't remember doing all those things? I remembered arriving home and drinking, but nothing after that. I knew I could scratch my head all day and not make sense of things. Plus, the problem that had caused my needing to become intoxicated was still out there. By now half the town knew about my family. I hated to think how many people were going to confront me about them and my feelings.

I had several missed calls from the station, as well as a few numbers that I didn't recognize. The clock on the microwave read eleven. I'd slept the whole damn day away.

Deciding not to push my luck, I called my deputy to see what all I had missed. Just like every day, it was pretty quiet. He had called me to make sure I was alright and let me know that a few people from town had called for me, including both of our two pastors.

I knew what they wanted.

They wanted to offer me counseling to help me get through my horrific ordeal. The pastor from where I'd lived before had offered me the same thing. Nothing was going to help me unless someone could raise the dead.

At close to midnight, I called it a night. There was no way that I was going to find anything to do to clear my mind and my head was pounding so bad that I just wanted to take some pills and sleep it off.

The next day I did go into work, except I locked myself in my office and did paperwork that I had procrastinated over. By the time that four came around, my stomach was growling something fierce. I needed a good, filling meal and there was only one place I knew to go for that.

Last Mile Bar and Grill may have had a new employee running the place, but the food was still just as good. I think Sue was still doing most of the cooking from home. When I walked inside, I spotted the good-looking blonde behind the bar. She looked up when she heard the door, but looked shocked to see me. It made no sense since we'd actually gotten along the last time I'd come in.

Figuring that she was just having a bad day, I headed toward the bar and sat down. This was far enough out of town where I never ran into anyone. It was also rundown and I think it scared most locals away. Since I was officially avoiding my town like the plague, this was the best place to be.

Vessa approached me with the same look on her face. "What's for dinner?"

"We went shopping today. You can have anything on the menu. I made a big pot of spaghetti if you like that." She refused to look at me. I didn't get it.

"You made it?"

A half smile formed in the corner of her lip. "Oh my word, am I dreaming or did you just say something funny?"

"It happens every once in a while." Truthfully, I couldn't even remember the last time I had made a joke for the purpose of making someone smile.

"I will have you know that I can cook pretty damn good. If you'd rather have a microwave hotdog, I'd be glad to get you one." She handed me a drink and waited for my comeback.

"I guess I can try the spaghetti, since you claim to be so good and all."

She let out an air-filled laughed as she shook her head and walked back into the kitchen. A couple minutes later, she came out with two plates of spaghetti. She sat one in front of me and slid the other one right beside it. Then she placed two sets of silverware down near the plates. I looked around, but didn't see anyone around that was waiting for food. It only took Vessa a second to make herself a soda and walk out from behind the bar to sit next to me.

She looked over and smiled as she grabbed her fork and took a bite. "Don't look at me like that. I'm starving and this is one of my favorites. If you need to take your plate over to your little corner, be my guest. I just thought it would be nice to not have to stand up and eat behind the bar."

I watched her take another bite and start chewing again. She opened her mouth with food still in it, to see how I would react. I shook my head and grabbed my own fork. It wasn't until I'd taken a couple bites that she put her fork down and stared at me. "What?"

"I just figured you'd get up. I don't know much about you, but I know you don't like company. I must be growing on you."

I didn't know if it was that or the fact that the whole world was closing in on me and she was the only person that wasn't judging me. I hadn't wanted a friend in a long time, but things had changed. My secret was going to spread throughout the town and eventually Sue and Vessa would know it too. For some reason, I wanted to be around her before she too felt sorry for me and pushed me away.

"I just wanted to be close to the bar when I died of food poisoning."

Vessa smacked me in the arm, making me laugh out loud. Her eyes got real big and she smiled too. "I had no idea that you had teeth. I mean, you never show them. I didn't think you knew how to smile, with all your hermit qualities."

She took her napkin and wiped her lips, but as she pulled away, I noticed something familiar about her mouth. When I thought she noticed what I was staring at, I turned my attention to my plate of food. "I always liked having this for dinner. My mom used to make these garlic knots that..."

"Oh shit!" Vessa went running into the kitchen.

I got up and followed behind her, taking her tone as a sign that something was wrong. By the time I got in there, she was waving a towel in front of a very smoky open oven. I could smell the garlic and realized what was going on. "Guess that's our garlic bread?"

"Damn, I made that from scratch. I can't believe I forgot about it. They're ruined now." She walked over to the counter and pulled out four slices of bread. "Guess this is the best I can do."

It was hard not to laugh at her. I'd been teasing her so much that she'd set herself up for another catastrophe. The thing was, smiling made me feel better about what was going on in my life. I wanted to be angry; to beat the shit out of something or go to the shooting range. Being around this woman settled me down. I just couldn't explain it.

I walked over and grabbed the pieces of bread, taking a bite in front of her. "If I was at home, I'd be eating Ramen noodles again. Your aunt has been feeding me dinner since I moved here. I have to say, she's one hell of a cook, but you are the first person to feed *and* entertain me."

She smacked me again on the arm. "Stop teasing me. I liked you better when you were just a douche."

"A douche? I've been called many things, but never a douche. Just because I don't like to socialize, doesn't mean I'm a douche."

Vessa picked at her bread. I watched her looking down, like she was confused. It was the same look from when she first saw me. "I don't get you. Ever since I moved here, you've made it clear that you didn't want friends. What changed in the matter of a day?"

I pinched my nose, feeling that burn when you first start to feel that migraine. "Would you rather me go back to not talking to you at all? I didn't say that I wanted to share life stories and shit."

She growled and started walking back out. "Whatever!"

When I followed her out, there still wasn't a single person in the bar. Tuesdays were slow. I liked coming in then because I was usually by myself. I sat down next to Vessa and finished my food in silence. When I pushed my plate out from in front of me, she stood up and grabbed both of them to carry to the kitchen.

Maybe this was a bad idea. I had no business trying to be friends with someone that had her own problems. That is when I realized it was because of her situation that I could relate to her. She too, was broken in her own way. It was also the reason why I couldn't be her friend.

I pulled out a twenty and sat it on the bar. While she was still in the back, I decided that it was better for me to just go. Obviously, she was confused about my actions and to be honest, I was too.

My hand pushed on the door for it to open. "You are seriously going to leave without saying goodbye?" She was standing with her hands on her hips.

"I enjoyed your cooking, Vessa, but I think it's best if I just go. I can't do this."

"Do what? We are two adults, Ramsey. I'm not asking for your damn hand in marriage. Look, I have no friends here. Like none! In fact, I don't have many friends back home either. I gave up my social life for the sake of my family. My life is so messed up, but when I'm working, I feel like I can breathe. My aunt is great and I am awfully grateful for her to take us in, but I need to be me once in a while."

"Why are you telling me this?"

"Because, maybe my aunt was right. Maybe we both need a friend." This was exactly what I didn't need. I had thought that this was the one place that I could come to for peace.

I looked down at the floor and thought about telling her that it was a bad idea. Just as I went to open my mouth and say it, something stopped me. I couldn't be mean to her for selfish reasons, no matter how much I wanted to just walk away. "I'm a terrible friend."

"Teach me how to play pool. I won't ask you anything unless I win a game. I don't even care if you talk to me. I just like the company."

I sighed. What could playing pool hurt? She wasn't pressing me about personal things and I kind of liked the company too. "This is a bad idea." I followed her over toward the pool table.

She grabbed a stick off the wall for herself and turned around to look at me. "My whole life has been bad ideas. I'm not afraid." I watched her bend over and take a shot at a ball that was just sitting on the table.

As the night progressed, so did my alcohol consumption. By my third drink, I was looking at Vessa in all the wrong ways. Try as she might, she still hadn't won a single game. Since I didn't have to answer any personal questions and I was pretty content with staring at her ass, I had her make me another drink.

A few people came in after we'd been playing for a while. When she went to go wait on them, I sat down and watched her working. I knew it was the alcohol making me think about her that way. Her full breasts filled out the fitted shirt she was wearing and her jeans left nothing for the imagination. She had to know how sexy she was, especially if she had always been a bartender. There was no way in hell that she didn't get hit on daily.

I closed my eyes and let myself imagine her being naked in front of me. I thought about having her sweet lips on parts of me that hadn't been touched in a long time. As I concentrated on what it would feel like to have her riding me, I heard someone clearing their throat. "You falling asleep on me?"

My eyes opened wide to see her standing in front of me with her hands on her hips. "No, ma'am. I was just resting my eyes."

"That couple just left, so it's just us again. How many questions are you up now?"

I lost count after seven. "About ten."

"I will answer two."

"That isn't what we agreed upon," I teased.

She hopped up on the pool table and sat on it, with her feet dangling. "What do you want to know about me, Sheriff?"

Right at that moment, I wanted to know things that I could never ask. "What is your husband like?"

She leaned back on the pool table and started to laugh. I didn't understand what was so funny, but at this point, I didn't understand much of anything.

"Why would you ask that? I think that is the weirdest question ever. He's a dick. He cheated on me over and over again and now some girl that is barely legal is carrying his child."

I could tell that she hated me for asking that. It was too late to take it back. "He's a fool."

She suddenly straightened up her body and looked at me. "I thought so too."

"He should have been focused on his kids instead of someone else. You never know when something bad could happen and you may never see them again." I paused, thinking about Katie and how much I wanted to say to her. Then I realized that I opened up a can of worms that I wasn't willing to explain. I stood up quickly and put my stick away. "I gotta go."

She hopped down and followed behind me. "Ramsey, wait! Are you okay?"

"Yeah, I just need to get my ass to bed."

"You've had a lot to drink. Do you want to wait and I will follow you home?"

"I'm fine!" I wasn't, though. For the past couple hours I had been thinking of how many ways I wanted to fuck her, all the while knowing that every second spent with her was only making my life worse.

I didn't look back as I headed for my truck, or when I pulled out of the parking lot.

Chapter 10

Vessa

I couldn't believe that he had come into the bar and acted like he hadn't just seen me. I mean, not only had I been at his place, but we'd also kissed. Now he was just going to come into the bar and act like nothing ever happened.

This guy was unreal!

It only took a little while for me to realize that it was possible that he had been too drunk to remember. As the night progressed, I was getting the feeling that Ramsey had no idea that he'd even left his house at all.

To say that it was for the best would have been an understatement. The last thing that either of us needed was for him to find out that I'd not only been in his house without permission, but also that I'd let him think I was his dead wife.

The kiss may have just been a memory for him, but it was something else for me. What started out as me just pretending, had turned into a moment of passion. It was something that I couldn't wrap my head around. Here was this guy that I barely knew anything about and yet I was obsessing over him like I was in high school.

I felt like I needed to help him; to fix him in some way. It wasn't like I expected him to want me in some kind of intimate way, but I did want him to trust me. He needed a real friend. Of course, if he knew about my lying, I was sure I'd be the last person on that list.

It was getting late, but a couple came in and ordered the special to eat. I served them a couple of drinks and then their food once it was heated. As they enjoyed each other's company, I started to clean up and prepare for the morning shift. My phone started ringing about halfway through what I was doing.

Hello?

It's your aunt. Listen, Logan is all upset. I tried to calm him down, but his father really got him upset over the phone.

What do you mean? What happened?

Well, you know that fishing trip that he promised him this weekend?

Yeah. Don't tell me he backed out? Logan has wanted to do that for two years now. How could he do that?

Claims he has something more important. If you ask me, I'd like to cut off his balls and feed them to a pack of pigs.

That would be hard to do since I am going to rip them off with my bare hands.

I just wanted you to know. Oh and if you haven't figured out, he can't take the kids at all this weekend either.

Okay, I am calling him right now!

I told you when you were in high school that he was loser.

I know. Everyone did!

See you at home, sweetie. Don't worry about Logan. He may still be upset, but it looks like he's finally fallen asleep.

Good. See you in a bit. I won't be late. It's slow tonight.

I didn't wait to calm down before I started calling Gavin's number. I was so damn pissed at the man. How could he think that standing up his kids was something that would be okay with me?

What do you want, Vessa?

Don't you even talk to me in that tone. How could you do this to Logan? Do you have any idea how important this was to him?

Things came up. It ain't like we can't do it another weekend.

You promised him this weekend. You only get them twice a month and you are already cancelling. What kind of father are you?

Don't be a bitch, Vessa. I've got other shit to do this weekend. I figured that you would be fine with it since you're so hell-bent on being mother of the year and shit.

Screw you, Gavin. I do my best to make sure our children are cared for. There isn't anything that I wouldn't do for them. Nothing is more important. Obviously we have much different opinions on parenting.

Jesus, all you ever do is nag. I don't know how I put up with that shit for as long as I did.

You rotten bastard! You lied and cheated and then are going to blame me for our failed marriage?

I cheated because of how you were. You just wait and see. I bet no man will ever want to be with you. There ain't no one that likes a woman with as many bitch qualities as you.

Oh, so I guess your little teenage slut is so much better?

I don't give a shit about her. There's plenty more where she came from.

You are an asshole. The biggest asshole I have ever met. If it were up to me, you wouldn't see your kids ever again. I hate you so much!

The feeling is mutual.

Go to Hell!

I just got out of it on the day you moved out!

Fuck you!

I hung up before he could say anything else that could rip out my heart. He had to have been drunk or on something to brutally treat me and the kids like we never meant anything to him. It still hurt so much. I didn't even want to think about how my poor boy was feeling. Neither one of the kids deserved to be ignored by their father. They loved him so much and just wanted to spend time with him.

I grabbed a bottle of Jack and poured a glass.

Jack and me didn't get along, but he was going to be my best friend until the pain went away.

I'd taken two shots when the couple came up and paid their bill. Since I was having a personal pity party, I decided to close up and get home before the alcohol started to hit. I cleaned up the dishes and made sure everything was turned off, before heading outside to my car.

Just as I was sticking my keys into the door, a set of headlights pulled into the lot, blinding me. I held my hand over my eyes, waiting to tell the person that we were closed. As I stood there, I heard the truck door close and saw a figure coming my way. In an instant, I was in a panic. It hadn't been that long ago that I'd been attacked by that drunken man. It could very well have been him coming toward me. The headlights of the truck were preventing me from seeing anything but a tall, dark figure.

My keys fell out of my hand and dropped to the ground as I backed up against my car. "We're closed!"

He kept approaching.

I backed up as far as I could get. After my phone call with Gavin, I wondered if he'd somehow found out where I was and sent someone to rough me up. "I have mace!" I turned around and reached in my purse to pull out the small container. It was probably expired, but it would scare him.

The man started to laugh at me. "If you mace me, you can forget about us being friends."

I felt his hand grabbing the container of mace out of my grasp. I knew who it was as soon as he'd spoke. I just couldn't believe that he was back. "Ramsey? You said you were going home."

"I headed that way, until I got a call about kids racing out of town. By the time I got to the location, they were long gone. I didn't know you'd be closing early."

"I didn't know you cared. Did you run out of booze at home?" I have no idea why I was being so rude. Perhaps it was the fact that he'd just scared the living shit out of me, right after I'd had it out with Gavin.

"It's all good. I can see that you're tired. I'll stop by another time."

He was finally acting like I didn't repulse him and I was giving him the cold shoulder, after I'd decided that I was going to be the supportive friend he needed. "Ramsey, wait!" He was starting to walk back to his truck. "I just had it out with my husband, well, my soon-to-be ex-husband. I didn't mean to snap. If you want to come in and shoot a couple games, it might give me some time to cool down."

He stood there for a second, just staring at me. It was too dark for me to be able to decipher what he was thinking. After his brief moment of silence, he started walking toward the door to the bar. "I think maybe you're the one that needs a drink now."

Once we got inside, I only turned on a couple of the lights. I didn't feel like waiting on any patrons that would assume the bar was still open. My aunt did most of her business on Friday, Saturday, and during the day shift, so the late night stragglers weren't that important. Mostly, they just caused drunken trouble.

Ramsey walked behind the bar, like he knew his way around. "You just take a seat. I'll get you something that will help you relax."

"I have to still drive home, you know." If this guy thought he could get me drunk, he was so wrong.

"One drink isn't going to kill you, Vessa."

"That's coming from someone that drinks all the time."

"I don't drink all the time. Some nights I like to unwind. My life is complicated. The alcohol helps me relax."

I wished that I could tell him that I knew about his family. I hated that I knew the truth. It was like I was lying to him. "My life sucks!" I grabbed the shot glass and let it pour down my throat. Ramsey leaned back against the bar wall and watched me.

"Because your husband?"

"Ex!" I shook my head and tapped on my glass. Ramsey started to fill it with more Bourbon. "He promised my son that he would take him fishing. The child has only wanted to go for the last two years. He was really looking forward to it. Out of nowhere, that asshole calls and says that they aren't going. Can you believe that? He stood up his own son."

Ramsey shook his head. "Some men don't know what they got. It doesn't take a rocket scientist to see that. It's a shame that your husband is…"

"Ex! We aren't together anymore."

"You know what I meant." I did know, but after everything that had happened, I wanted nothing to do with the liar.

"I'm glad you came back." My reply was both in a whisper and timid. I was actually scared to talk to Ramsey this way.

He cleared his throat and seemed to have to think about how to respond to me. "How bout that pool game?"

Ahh, he wasn't going to answer me. It was okay. I got it. I just hated that this man could be holding in his demons and not letting anyone in to help him. It made me want to help him even more. Except, with my own set of problems, it made me seem like I was the one who needed the help. I was pretty sure that Ramsey was only coming around me now because he pitied my situation. Why else would this broken man want to spend a single second with a still married, mother of two? "Sure."

Just like the games before them, I let Ramsey take the lead. He played in a way that made me think that maybe, just maybe, he was showing off a bit. He played the game well and I loved watching it. I'd seen quite a lot of people play pool in my lifetime and there was just something graceful about the way he held that stick in his hands. It was like the gentle side of Ramsey Towers was peeking out of the hermit façade.

He ran out a few of his balls on the table before giving me a turn. "Your shot. Do you remember how to play?"

I laughed and leaned over the table. "Pretty sure."

Since I had been the one serving Ramsey earlier, I knew that he'd had a bunch to drink, but the man standing before me seemed collected and far from being drunk. I suppose he really did handle his alcohol. It also reminded me of how sad and lonely his life must be to only have a bar to come to, instead of a friend.

Here I was, pretending that I couldn't shoot, just to get to know him better. I'd really stooped low this time. Not to mention the fact that I was still legally married. My husband may have been a total douche, but on paper, he was my douche.

In all honestly, Ramsey was the first man that I had ever really been attracted to, other than Gavin. I'm not meaning like some guy that just looked good when he walked by or ordered a drink. I'm talking the kind of attraction where I was dying to know what made him tick. Perhaps it was just the whole mysterious vibe that he wore on his sleeve. There was so much more to Ramsey. Whether he wanted me to know or not, I was going to find out.

We played three games before he said something other than pool tips. A few times, I found myself biting my tongue to prevent myself from laughing. I wanted to turn around and contradict him.

Ramsey did a great job talking to someone without having a single personal detail revealed. He didn't ask and neither did I. After three games, he walked over and got me another drink. By this time, I was already feeling a little too relaxed. I usually never drank, because when I did, I couldn't shut up.

I knew I was leaning over the table, laughing and acting all giddy, but at the same time, he was smiling more. His teeth were almost perfect except he had one crooked canine on the left side. The stubble on his face must have grown pretty quickly, since he had a five o'clock shadow almost every night that I'd seen him. Don't get me started on those matching tattoos that I wasn't even supposed to know about. When he bent over, I found myself watching to see if his underwear were hanging out the top of his pants. If someone was watching me from afar, they would have thought I was just plain creepy.

When he handed me the drink, he opened his bottle of water and took a long sip. I too sipped on my drink. "You feel any better?"

I nodded. "Alcohol can't be the answer to my problems. I need to just face them."

His jaw clenched and I could tell that my comment seemed like I was insinuating that alcohol was the answer to his problems. "I never said it was the answer, but it does take the edge off. Sometimes, I just don't feel like caring."

"Well, that is pretty obvious. I'm a good listener, you know. I mean, this is as close to having a friend as I'm going to get. So, if you need something, anything, just tell me."

He let out an air-filled laugh and shook his head. "I can tell that aside from your husband, you really don't have much experience talking to men."

"What's that supposed to mean?" I put my hands on my hips and waited for his answer.

He turned to face me, moving his body closer to where I stood. When I looked up into his eyes, I wasn't sure if I was afraid or turned on. "It means that you can't offer a man something, or anything." He raised his eyebrows, waiting for me to get what he was saying.

"Oh. Oh! I wasn't suggested that… I mean…"

He laughed again. "It's fine. I know what you meant. I've already told you that I don't talk about my life. It's nothing personal, Vessa." I sat down and basically pouted. I wasn't crying or acting like a baby with my lip out, but I just looked down at my drink and avoided eye contact. He sat across from me and waited for me to look up at him. "It has nothing to do with you. If it makes you feel any better, I haven't hung out with anyone like we are right now. I am a terrible excuse for a friend, but I suppose if you really like my company, you know where to find me."

"Friendship goes both ways, you know. We can't be friends if I know nothing about you. I mean, wasn't that the reason that we were playing pool, to get to know each other?"

"I didn't say that, you did."

"You knew what it implied. I wouldn't have played you if I didn't want to know you. Whatever it is, you can tell me." I reached my hand over and touched his.

Right away, he pulled away from me. "Don't! Sorry. I should get you home now."

I held up my glass. "You just made me drink liquor. I can't drive home."

"I'll drive you home, Vessa. Then I will have someone get the car to you in the morning. Consider it my part in this new friendship that you want so much." Ramsey stood up and grabbed his keys out of his pocket. He leaned over and took the glass from me, then walked it over to the sink and cleaned it.

After we turned off all the lights, we both headed toward the door. At the same time, both of our hands grabbed the doorknob. His warm hand was underneath mine. Bravery wasn't my strong point, except when alcohol was involved. I scooted myself in between him and the door. Our faces were almost touching. When he tried to pull away, I squeezed his hand. "Kiss me."

His eyes got big enough that I could see the white in them, even in the dark. "Vessa, that is the alcohol talking. Trust me, you don't want that."

I didn't let go. I held my body close to his and let my lips brush over his. I was surprised that he didn't fight me. He just held his body still. "My ex told me that no man would ever want me again. Don't tell me what I want."

It was clear to me at that moment that this was the first time since losing his wife that Ramsey had been in this position. He was weak and I was taking advantage of that. "We need to get you home," he said as our lips made contact again.

"Just kiss me." My other hand reached up and grabbed the collar to his shirt, pulling him into my lips. I opened my eyes and saw that he'd closed his. In a matter of just seconds, what started as light pecks turned into a full-blown make-out session. His breathing increased, as did mine, while our tongues mingled. He pulled his hand away from mine and grabbed my hair. I kissed his cheek with my lips and a slip of my tongue. The stubble tickled me, but made him release a low groan.

When my hands began to move around, he grabbed both of my arms and pulled away. His lips were on my forehead. "We need to stop."

I nodded, knowing that this was as far as it was going to go. As hot as I was between my legs, I knew we weren't going to sleep together.

We said nothing on the ride to my aunt's house. I didn't know what to say to him. Our second kiss had felt even better than the first. After both times, there was only one thing that I knew for sure.

I wanted more of Ramsey Towers.

Chapter 11

Ramsey

She was under my skin now and I wasn't sure if I wanted her there. Don't get me wrong, sexually, she was definitely a weakness. I wasn't a fool. I knew that my wife was gone, but as far as moving on, well, I'd never even considered it. Because of me, they'd lost their lives. It wasn't fair for me to want to be happy again.

I can't say that I hadn't thought about her puffy lips and what they would feel like against mine. Hell, I'd thought about a whole lot more than that when it came to Vessa. In the short time that I'd known her, she'd made me open up more than I had since the accident.

It also meant that it made me feel guilty over my actions.

I didn't want Vessa to feel like she wasn't attractive. She needed to know that her husband cheated because he couldn't keep his shit in his pants. She was stunning. Everything about the woman had the potential to get my blood flowing. Unfortunately, I wasn't going to go there. This friendship that she wanted was going to have to end. I couldn't continue to get close to her.

In no time at all, I fell asleep on the couch. Just like every night, my dream was more of a memory. I'd just come off a long shift where we had a double homicide. The family had been at the scene and it was just hard not to bring that kind of shit home with me.

I found my girls asleep on the couch. They were covered up with a small throw blanket. Quietly, I made my way to the chair across from them and started to remove my boots. It was difficult not to wake up Jules. She was the lightest sleeper that I'd ever known. Her eyes opened and she caught me watching her.

I think right away she knew that it hadn't been a good night for me. After being a cop's wife for a while, she just knew. She scooted herself off the couch, without waking Katie, and then made her way over to my chair. Jules said nothing as she climbed up into my lap, straddling me. Her lips found mine and I accepted the only cure for my shitty night.

Her erotic tongue moved with unique technique. I was always a sucker to her seduction skills. She was like that Bon Jovi song, Bad Medicine. Her dark hair was pulled back and I took it upon myself to free it from the clip, so that I could see her waves fall down over her shoulders.

Realizing that our daughter could wake up at any moment, Jules climbed off me and grabbed my hand, pulling me up the stairs with her. I followed like a little puppy, waiting for a reward for being a good boy.

While she went into the bathroom for a moment to herself, I started ripping off my clothes. I didn't want to waste a single second when she came out. Our mattress was new and a pillow top, so I flopped down on it and closed my eyes while I waited for her to join me.

She came out wearing nothing, just the way I wanted it. Her slow strut to the bed was tantalizing, exactly how she wanted it to be. "Give me a number." This was how Jules and I discussed my night's work. It was a scale of ten being the worst and one being an easy night with no occurrences.

"Nine," I said while watching her climb on top of me.

She ran her hands up my chest and bit down on her lip. "Kids?"

"Teens. Parents came to the scene," I whispered between kisses.

Jules sat up and rocked her body back and forth. Her movements made me crazy considering that my dick was already rock hard. I grabbed her hips and flipped her underneath of me. She gasped, but quickly went back to seducing me with her sweet kisses.

I entered her slowly, allowing her to accept my girth. Her legs wrapped around mine, like a pretzel. I watched her face as we began to grind together. She leaned into my chest and licked at my nipple, while I ran my hands up and down her fine ass. Low sounds of pleasure filled the room as we continued our late night therapy session of making love.

The harder I pumped my erection into her, the more she grinded her body into me. I cupped her breasts and pinched her little nipples as she was about to come. Her body bucked and, at the same time, I reached down and rubbed her clit hard. She put the pillow over her mouth to prevent waking up our daughter as she let out a scream. Her body fell flat against the soft mattress.

I halted my movements, giving her a couple seconds to recover, before I spun her around and pounded my final moments of stress out. She knew just what I wanted too. Jules turned around, got on all fours, and put her perfect ass up in the air. I watched her reach down and touch herself, showing me she wasn't done either. The invitation was not wasted as once again we came together.

I loved the way it sounded in this position. Our bodies slapped together with each thrust; my balls slapping against her sensitive sex. I dug my hands into her hips and pulled her into me until finally I felt my release filling her. Her pussy clenched and tightened, letting me know she was yet again having another orgasm.

We collapsed on the bed together, only for a short moment, on account of her having to go get cleaned up. I stood up and put on my underwear, in order to carry our daughter up to her room. I knew she wouldn't wake up, but I didn't want to take the chance of her being devastated forever.

When I climbed back into bed is when I realized that something about my memory had changed. The atmosphere in the room felt different. I got under the covers and reached over to put my arms around Jules, except when she turned around it wasn't my wife.

Vessa was lying next to me, in my bed, with no clothes on. Her hair was messed up and she had a big smile on her face. She took her finger and traced over my lips. "I missed you."

I sat straight up on the couch and looked around the room. It was dark and all I could hear were the crickets outside. Call it my guilty conscience, but I was freaked out. From the reaction, I got up and started pacing around. Up until this very night, they'd all been special memories of my old life.

Something was happening to me and Vessa was the reason. I couldn't let her taint my memories of them, even if she wasn't meaning to do that. How could she? It wasn't like I had divulged my life story to her. It didn't even matter. I needed to distance myself from her. I wasn't willing to take the chance of losing the only thing I had left of them.

Some things are easier said then done though. The next morning was my official day off. Now being the sheriff, a day off really meant that I was able to do personal things until something came up that needed my attention. I'd planned on cleaning off the metal roof and raking up all the winter leaves that had accumulated. I didn't care what the yard looked like, but it kept my mind off things.

I'd no sooner gotten out the rake and the ladder when my phone started ringing. Of course, I shook my head before answering—knowing damn well it was going to be work.

I was wrong.

A familiar, raspy voice was on the other end.

Ramsey, it's Sue. Listen, I need a man favor.

Is there anyone else you can call?

Not particularly. Why? Did I do something to offend you?

No. What do you need?

It would be easier if you would come by.

You at the bar?

Nope, I switched with Vessa. I'm home today.

Be there shortly.

As long as I didn't have to see Vessa, I figured I would be in the clear, as far as giving the old lady a hand. She probably just needed me to fix something around her place. I don't know how I'd been designated as her personal go-to, but I didn't mind. Before Vessa, she'd been the only person that I could tolerate being around. In some ways I think she looked out for me.

After grabbing my tools, I headed over to Sue's place. I had my mind set on whatever the task was she needed me to do. The little boy, Logan, came running toward my car. "Hey, Sheriff. You got your gun today?"

I patted him on the head. "I'm off today, kid. Where's your aunt?"

"She's inside."

I continued to walk past him, heading for the front door. Sue was sitting in the kitchen with a cookbook in her hand. I cleared my throat so that she would know it was me and not the kid. "That was fast. You want some coffee? I just made another pot."

"Sounds good!" The coffee pot at the cabin hadn't been used. The whole kitchen hadn't been used. I was used to buying my coffee in town every morning. Actually, I got it for free for being the sheriff, but always tipped whatever it cost anyway.

I sat down across from Sue, waiting for her to tell me just what she called me over to do. She marked the book with a dog-ear and looked up at me. "Like I said on the phone. I need a favor."

"I brought my tools. Just tell me what needs fixing."

She gave me an inquisitive stare. "This ain't something that requires tools. I am going to ask you this because I know she won't and I wouldn't even consider it, if I didn't know how important it was to the boy."

"I am afraid you lost me."

"Take him fishing, Ramsey. I don't even care if it's only for an hour. I just need you do it."

I was floored. Not only was she asking me for something personal, but it was also a favor for the one person in town that I was trying to avoid. "It's a bad idea."

"The kid's good-for-nothing father promised to take him, and then decided to have a weekend with his girlfriend instead. Slowly but surely, he's going to stop seeing them kids all together. I don't know what Vessa is going to do about it. Look, my sister passed away a while back and, for a while, Vessa kept her distance. Having them in my life is more important to me than anything. She won't ask for help, but I'm determined to do it anyway."

"I'm not good with kids." It was a lie. Every kid reminded me of my daughter and it was brutally painful for me.

"It's one hour. It ain't like he is going to pry into your business. If he get's curious, make something up. If you ask me, it would do you both a load of good."

"I have to work."

"I already called the station. I know you're off today. Look, you take the kid fishing and I will send you home with a chicken pot pie. Don't tell me that you don't love it. I've seen you tear through my pot pies before."

She had a point. The woman knew how to feed me. She also knew how to push my buttons. One thing that I was sure of was that she wasn't going to back down. "One hour, Sue."

"There are old rods in the shed and the pond should be crazy full of fish, since my Ray stocked it before he died. If you catch it, you can keep it. I will fry it up some way or another." She opened the cookbook and started looking at what she was looking at before I came into the room.

"You want me to go now?"

"Why not?"

I shook my head and walked out of the kitchen. The kid was sitting on the step where I'd left him. He had a baseball glove in his hand and was throwing the ball up and catching it. Half the time he would miss and have to get up to retrieve it.

I didn't look at him when I spoke. "Follow me, kid."

He caught up with me fast. "Where we going? You taking me on a ride along? I saw it on TV last night."

It was going to be the longest hour of my life. "I'm taking you fishing, kid. You're too young for a ride along." He stopped following me, so I turned around to see what happened. He just stood there, looking down at the ground. "What's wrong, kid?"

"My name is Logan, not kid, and my dad was supposed to take me fishing." He seemed pissed off.

I struggled with myself over what actions I should take. On one hand, I would have liked to get in my truck and head home without having to burden myself with the whole ordeal. On the other hand, I saw a kid that had his heart broken by someone he counted on. He needed to know that not everyone was going to disappoint him. I shook my head and cussed under my breath for what I was about to do.

Without arguing myself out of it, I knelt down in front of him. "Listen here, Logan. I'm going into the shed and grabbing two rods. Then I'm going to walk down to that pond and fish for a while. I don't know what you had planned for the day, but the company would sure be nice. It's up to you though."

It didn't take but a second for him to catch up to me walking away. I didn't say anything else, even when we got to the shed and grabbed the rods and tackle.

Logan had never been fishing, so I had to teach him how to bait his hook and cast his line. I have to give him credit for trying. He listened to my every word. After attempting to cast four times on his own, I took the line and cast it out for him. He smiled as we sat next to each other on the little man-made pier. His little feet were swinging around while he tightly held the rod, waiting for his bobber to disappear out of the water.

"You having fun, kid, err, Logan?"

"How long does it take to catch one?" He didn't answer my question. I figured he would get bored fast. I remember how it was to fish with my father when I was a kid.

"I've fished a whole week without a bite."

"Maybe you aren't good at it. I bet my dad could catch a big fish real fast."

I bit my tongue, but I gotta admit, it was real hard to do. After hearing just a few things that the guy had done, I was sure that his ass had no balls, or compassion for his wife or kids. Unfortunately, this kid was too young to understand all that, and as I learned more about his mother, I learned that her compassion for her children had caused her to keep negative things about their father from them. The more I wanted to avoid the woman, the more I respected the kind of person she was.

Thankfully, my bobber went down into the water. I knew what I had to do, when I turned to see the look on Logan's face. I handed the kid my rod. "Pull it in, Logan. This fish is going to be your catch."

He reeled his little heart out, trying to pull in that fish. Now, when Sue told me that her deceased husband had stocked the pond, I hadn't considered how large those fish would have gotten. After fighting for five minutes, I stood behind Logan to help him pull the fish in. I think we both were in shock, when we pulled up a bass that was nearly two feet in length. With giant eyes, the kid watched me use the net and get the fish out of the water. Once it was in the bucket, we smacked hands at our catch. "It's giant!"

I was proud of him. Sadly, it reminded me of another moment that I would never get to share with Katie. As depressing as it was for me, I patted the kid on the shoulder. "Let's try to catch some more. I'm thinking our bait is too small for what's swimming around in this pond. We should try something else on our lines."

"Can we catch a shark?"

"If there's a shark in this pond, we're both going to have to change our pants." I knew there wasn't, but the kid seemed to think it was the coolest thing ever.

He watched me bait his line. "Why would we change our pants? Are we going to fall in? I don't want to fall in with the sharks."

I started laughing—not even considering what I'd told him could scare him. "I meant that if there was a shark in this little pond, I was going to crap my pants."

He giggled. "You poop yourself? Only babies poop themselves."

Clearly, sarcasm wasn't in his vocabulary. "Never mind. How about we talk about something else?" That's when it happened. I'd opened myself up to the boy, while sitting on that pier. After nearly a year of solitude, I'd opened myself up to a curious kid.

"My dad said that after we caught fish, we could go out for ice cream." I clenched my jaw, knowing the kid was trying to get something extra out of me. The thing was, I kind of liked being around him. He was too young to judge me, or understand why I was the way I was around other adults.

"Let's see how many we can catch first." That's what we did too. For the next couple hours, we sat around talking about baseball, bugs, and fighting crime. He never asked me anything that made me feel uncomfortable.

When we got finished, we'd brought in seven large fish. Sue was outside hanging laundry when we came across the field with what we'd caught. She put down a shirt and walked toward us. "How'd you do?"

Logan pointed to the filled bucket.

She looked from him to me and smiled. "You know what this means?"

The little kid was as confused as me. "No?"

"It means that you and the sheriff have a lot more fish to catch. Maybe this is something that you can do again."

She kept smiling when she winked at me. This wasn't part of her favor, but after spending the majority of the day with Logan, I'd realized that I had relaxed and enjoyed myself. "Maybe so."

"We have to get these fish in the house, so that we can have ice cream," he explained.

"I don't know if we have any ice cream," she admitted.

He got a sad look on his face. I sat down the heavy load of fish. "Looks like we are going to have to go into town then."

"Let me change my shirt. Be right back!" he yelled as he ran into the house.

"You did a real good thing today, Ramsey." I could tell that she was up to something.

Just like her pushing me toward Vessa, I figured it out almost immediately. "You did this on purpose, didn't you?"

"Don't know what you're talking about. I just wanted the kid not to be damaged because he's got a daddy that doesn't give a damn."

"So, it had nothing to do with trying to get me to open up?" She was a clever woman, with apparent tricks up her sleeve.

"Why? Is that what's happening?" She was acting all dumb about it.

I shook my head, knowing that I was caught in another one of her plans. "For someone that doesn't pry, you sure seem to be involved in my actions, more than ever."

"I know a broken man when I see one. It doesn't take a genius to know that you've been through something. I'd never ask what it was. I'm not that type of woman. You need to know that all broken men can be fixed."

"You can't fix me, Sue. Nobody can fix me." Not when I wished that I had died in that car with my family. I was dead to society and didn't want to be apart of it anymore.

"You keep telling yourself that. Mark my word, Ramsey. Things are about to change for you. You'll see."

I shook my head, getting exactly what she was saying. "You need to stop trying to push us together. It's never going to happen with your niece, Sue."

"I saw you drop her off last night. Looks like you've been spending time together, if you asked me. Everyone needs friends, you know. The best ones come into your life when you aren't looking for them."

I was tired of hearing it from her, but my parents brought me up to respect my elders, so I kept my mouth shut. It was a good thing, because Logan came running outside in clean clothes. "I'm ready. Can we turn on the siren?"

Sue had already picked back up on hanging her clothes. "I'll bring him back in a little while."

"Take your time. I'm sure Vessa would love for you to stay for dinner."

She had to give her two cents again. I walked close to her so that the kid couldn't hear me. "I drove Vessa home because she'd been drinking, and as a police officer, I couldn't allow her to do that. Nothing is going to happen between the two of us. I can be cordial to your niece, but nothing has changed. I don't need friends like you think. I manage just fine!"

Without hearing what she said back to me, I walked away from her and headed to the truck, where Logan waited patiently. Spending the day fishing with the kid was one thing, but being set up with someone that I was determined to avoid was not.

Chapter 12

Vessa

The day shift was busy. It kept me from thinking about my intimate moments with Ramsey the night before. Since alcohol was involved, I couldn't be too sure how he was going to react to it all. My luck, he'd stay away and not talk to me for months.

By the time my shift was over, all I wanted to do was lay around with the kids and relax. My hangover was kicking my ass. You can imagine what it was like when my aunt pulled up to switch places with me and one of my kids wasn't in the car. "Where's Logan?"

I could tell she was up to something. My aunt and my mother shared several qualities. This was one of them. "He's with the sheriff."

I put my hands on my hips and looked over at her. "What are you talking about? Why is he with him? What happened?"

"Just go home and have a nice night, Vessa. Logan is fine. In fact, I assure you he is better than fine."

I didn't ask her what she did. I just wanted to get home and see my son. Being on my own for the first time made me nervous. If something bad happened, I was scared that Gavin could take custody of them, whether he wanted them or not. He would do it to spite me.

Asha didn't say much. She was in the backseat with her headphones on her ears. Not that she would have cared where her brother was, anyway. She looked forward to him being away from her.

When we pulled up at the house, I didn't see Ramsey's truck. It made me nervous. I rushed into the kitchen and found his number on the refrigerator. It rang four times and went to voicemail. I tried two more times, before hearing a truck pulling into the driveway.

The frustration of not knowing had already taken over, and by the time that Ramsey stepped out of his truck, I was already at it, screaming. "How could you just take my kid without my permission?"

"It wasn't a big deal, Vessa. Your aunt knew all about it."

"I don't care about my aunt. When it comes to my kids, you ask me, not her!"

He looked over at the passenger side of the truck; I could see that Logan was still buckled in the seat. "Look, the kid had a good day. Can't you just be happy without blowing this whole thing out of proportion? I was doing you a damn favor."

"I didn't ask for a favor! My God, you've probably been drinking." My hands were still on my hips.

"I knew this was a bad idea." He shook his head and walked away from me.

I could see him getting Logan unhooked. Sure enough, my little guy came running from around the other side of the truck. "Mommy! Mommy, the sheriff took me fishing. We caught lots of big ones. Then he took me to get ice cream, just like dad was going to. Can the sheriff eat dinner with us?"

At the same time, Ramsey and I both yelled, "No!"

My son's bottom lip came out. "But why not?"

I leaned down to look at him. "Go get all that ice cream washed off your face. I'll be inside in a minute."

Before I could even understand what was happening, Logan ran over to Ramsey and hugged him at the waist. "Thanks for the best day ever. Sorry my mom is being a meanie." Then he ran into the house.

I threw my hands into the air. "Great! Now I'm the bad guy."

Ramsey leaned against his truck. He pulled off his hat and ran his hands through his thick hair. "Listen, I think it's best if I just head home. I get why you're mad, Vessa, but you need to know that I would never put a child in harm's way. I'm pissed that you think I would be drinking."

I covered my face. "I'm sorry. I know I am overreacting. I just didn't know and with Gavin being such a bastard, I have to be careful."

"Look, I was going to suggest that we stop what's been going on anyway. I told you from the beginning that I wasn't the kind of guy you wanted to be friends with. It's obvious that this isn't going to work. You have problems and I'm not the man that everyone thinks I am. It's for the best." Ramsey turned to climb into his truck.

My heart began beating out of my chest. I don't know what it was, but I began to sob. This wasn't me playing games with him to get him to open up. This was me desperately trying to not lose whatever I was feeling for this man. I rushed up next to him and put myself between him and the truck. He backed away and held up his hands. "I'm sorry. Don't be like this, Ramsey. I don't want you to go."

I knew he was telling me goodbye. Not the kind of goodbye, like I would be seeing him around. He was closing the doors back up. "You need to know that you're a beautiful woman. If things were different, maybe I could have showed you the way you deserve to be treated."

I kept shaking my head as the tears fell down my face. "I know what you're doing. Don't shut me out, Ramsey. I want to be your friend."

He looked away, perhaps to think of what to say without having to hurt my feelings so much. I closed my eyes, realizing that I had no control of what his decision was going to be. I felt his hand brush across my face and wipe away the tears. "Don't cry on my account. I'll never hurt you again. Just tell the kid that I got a call. He'll think it was cool and let you off the hook about it." He moved me out of the way and finally got into his truck. With the ignition started, he turned and looked down at me. "I'll never be what you want me to be, Vessa. I'm broken and there is no way to be fixed."

He backed out of the driveway and left before I could say anything else to him. I didn't understand what had gotten into me. He was just a man. I barely knew him. Sure, I knew more than he thought, but was it really enough to get myself all worked up about? Was I crying because I failed at being his supportive friend?

Maybe he hated me for asking him to kiss to me.

For someone that wanted to avoid men, I'd gone and gotten myself infatuated with one.

After the devastation wore off, I was left standing in my driveway alone. I ran into the house and called the bar.

She must have recognized the number as her house.

If you're calling to yell at me, save it. I'm too busy right now.

Why did you let Ramsey take Logan today without my permission? I knew I shouldn't have told him about Gavin last night. I need to keep my mouth shut.

I really hope you weren't too hard on him. I had to really beg him to take the child this morning. He was completely against the idea.

What do you mean? It wasn't his idea?

Of course it wasn't. Think about who were are talking about here. Ramsey Towers doesn't volunteer to be sociable, well, not unless it means he gets a meal out of it.

Oh no!

What do you mean, oh no?

I have to go. I'll see you tonight.

I didn't wait for her to ask for details. My aunt, who also thought she was a matchmaker, had been the one to set everything up, not Ramsey. I'd chewed him out and accused him of being drunk when he'd been doing something out of the kindness of his heart. It was no wonder that he wanted nothing more to do with me. I was so ashamed.

Of course, I couldn't leave the children unattended and Ramsey finding out that I knew where he lived wasn't going to go over well. After running down the street, I managed to talk the teenager two doors down to babysit for me. Her family attended our local church and she had volunteered her services when I first moved in. I gave her my cell phone number, kissed the kids, ordered a pizza, and ran out the door.

I don't even remember driving to Ramsey's cabin, but as I pulled in I realized that I had no idea what to say to the man. As soon as I climbed out of my car, I heard his porch door opening and saw him coming out of his house. His shirt was unbuttoned, but from the look in his eyes, I knew he didn't care. "Vessa, what are you doing here? How did you find where I lived?"

I played with the keys in my hand, afraid to look him in the eyes.

He walked right up to me. "Nobody knows where I live. Tell me how you found me."

I refused once more to look at him. He took his hand and reached for my chin, forcing me to look at him. "A couple nights ago you came into the bar in bad shape."

"What are you talking about?"

This was it. I had to tell him the truth. I couldn't keep it from him anymore. "Can we go inside and talk?"

He hesitated before waving his hand in the direction of the porch. Once inside, I sat down on the couch. He stood over me, like a pissed off dad when you broke curfew. "Vessa, you need to start explaining how in the hell you found me and I don't want some made up story."

I put my hands on my knees and looked down at the floor, while taking a few deep breaths. It wasn't like we were vested in a relationship. Ramsey had made it clear that he wanted nothing to do with me. I had nothing to lose. "You came into the bar already intoxicated. We were slow that night and I couldn't let you drive yourself home. I managed to take your keys and eventually you were able to show me where you lived. Once we arrived here, I got you situated in your bed and straightened up for you. Then I had my aunt pick me up so you wouldn't be mad at me and accuse me of prying. I swear I was just trying to help you. You were in no shape to drive."

He took his hat off and threw it on the chair beside us. "You know, don't you?"

I caught him glancing at the stack of papers that had been in his truck. He looked back at me and I was sure all the color left my face. "Yes. I saw them in your truck that night."

Ramsey put his head down. There was no expression on his face. It was like he was dead. "You need to leave."

I stood up and walked toward the door. With my hand on the doorknob, I turned around and saw him standing in the same position. "Did you think that I would act different if I knew the truth?"

"Vessa, don't do this. I appreciate you taking me home, but we can't be friends, not now, not ever."

I pushed the door shut and walked back toward him. "What are you so afraid of? I just want to help."

"You can't help me. No one can. Don't you get it? Nothing can change what happened. Nothing can bring them back." He picked up a wooden duck and threw it against a wall.

It terrified me, but for some reason, I knew he wasn't going to hurt me. For probably what was the first time, he was letting his feelings out. "I'm not leaving!" I plopped back down on the couch and watched him give me a dirty look.

When he wouldn't look at me anymore, I picked up one of the papers and started rereading the article. He walked over and grabbed it out of my hand like it was sacred. "Please just leave, Vessa."

I stood up and approached him from behind, reaching my arms around him. He stood there still and when he tried to pull away, I held him tighter. Try as he may, I continued to hold him. Finally, sensing my intentions, I felt his hands covering over mine. Quiet sniffles filled the room, and his body began to shake. I knew what was happening, so I stayed still, letting my head rest on his back as he let out what he'd been hiding from the whole world. For a few minutes he would play with my fingers and then he'd keep them still for a few more.

After some time had passed, he turned around, forcing me to let go of my hold on him. His eyes were red and his face was soaked with his emotional breakdown. He said nothing, so I grabbed him by the hand and we sat down on the couch side by side. I could tell that he didn't want to talk. I kept his hand in mine and put my other hand over it.

Ramsey caught me off guard when he started talking. "It was cold that night. We'd just left a party at one of our new neighbors' houses. The snow was falling when we left, but I was certain that I could get us home safe." He paused and wiped his face again with his opposite hand. "I promised Katie that we could build a snowman in the morning. We were talking about decorating it, and in a matter of seconds, they were gone. They were right next to me, Vessa. I cried out to them, over and over and they wouldn't answer me. My body was pinned down and I couldn't see them. I told the people to save them first. I told them to let me go." He began to cry again. "I killed them, Vessa. My wife and daughter died because of me."

"It's not your fault. Ramsey, it was a terrible accident. You can't blame yourself for what happened that night."

He looked up with eyes full of tears. "They died because of me. Katie never got to build that snowman." He stood up and kicked the table. "All she wanted was a fucking snowman." Ramsey's knees got weak and he sat back down beside me. This time, I pulled his head onto my chest and let him cry. I could feel his warm tears running down my skin.

To be honest, I'd never seen a grown man so overcome by emotions. Gavin had cried the first time I wanted to separate, but it didn't compare to this situation. I ran my hands through the hair that I had fantasized about for weeks, except it was for comfort instead of a turn on.

Once he had finally calmed down enough, he got up and went to the bathroom. When he finally came out, he leaned against the wall and looked right at me. I'd folded my hands and was just sitting there, wondering what in the hell had got me to this very moment. "Are you okay?"

He shrugged.

"I've been better."

"I'm sorry I didn't tell you that I knew. I wanted you to tell me yourself."

"That probably never would have happened, especially since I said I never wanted to see you again. The thing is, you were bound to find out. It was only a matter of time before Sue found out and told you. Word travels through small towns." He sat back down next to me, but looked forward. "I didn't want your pity. I know what happened that night. I just can't hear one more person tell me how sorry they are. They have no idea what it's been like for me. I couldn't face it. It's why I moved out here in the first place."

"I won't tell anyone. The news will blow over anyway. In a few weeks there will be some teenager knocked up by the pastor's son, or something."

An air-filled chuckle escaped him. "Maybe. They will still know though."

"Did you really think that you could live out the rest of your life without anyone knowing?" I reached out for his hand, but he pulled away.

"Honestly?"

I nodded. "Of course."

"For the longest time, I didn't want to live. I didn't get why God was punishing me, keeping me here. I mean, how could he let them die and keep me alive? They were so innocent. They didn't deserve to die."

"My mother died a while back. She was my very best friend. It wasn't an accident that took her. It was cancer. Anyway, the reason I am telling you this is because, right before she died, I said the same thing. She told me that this life on earth was just a test for us to go to heaven. She said that the true at heart die young because they don't need to live the trial like others. I thought it was just her medication making her say things, but after she passed, I looked around the hospital at all of those young children battling cancer. That's when I understood what she was saying and started to believe it myself. I don't know what you believe, Ramsey, and maybe saying this might make you hate me even more, but I have to believe that your girls are in a better place. They'd want you to be happy in this life, for however long you have it. You'll see them again one day and all the time that has passed will mean nothing."

He smiled, but remained quiet for a moment. We sat in silence.

I was pretty certain he was going to pick me up and carry me outside to my car.

Instead, he grabbed my hand and started playing with it. "You're the first person that I've talked to about this. Your mom sounds like a great woman. I can see how her and Sue were sisters. They have a way with people, don't they?"

"That they do."

"Can I ask you something?"

I smiled and watched him playing with my hand. "Anything."

"Was last night our first kiss?"

I felt shamed again. He was starting to remember little details and, of course, that was one of the first to come back to him. "I think you know the answer."

"I don't remember much. I went into work that morning like every other day. When I found out that the paper had printed that article, I left and bought every damn copy that I could find. That's when I started hitting the bottle so hard. Please tell me that I didn't make a fool out of myself. Did I hurt you or try to do something that you didn't want to do?"

I almost laughed out loud. "Of course not! It was wrong of me to let you think I was your wife. I know you never would have kissed me otherwise. You were just so messed up and I didn't want you to get upset. I had no idea how you would react. Besides, do you really think I would have wanted to kiss you the next day if you hurt me in any way? Ramsey, I… I just want us to be friends. I like you… more than I probably should be admitting."

He finally turned his body and faced me. My hand was still in his. He looked down at it and then scrunched up his face, like he was in pain. "I like you too, Vessa. That's why we shouldn't be friends."

"I don't understand."

"Every time I look at you, I feel like I'm cheating on my wife."

There was nothing that I could say to that. I couldn't talk my way out of it. So instead of saying something that could hurt his feelings, or my own, I just sat there.

"I don't want to hurt you. I know you have enough on your plate," he replied.

"I didn't plan on falling for you, Ramsey." Tears were forming and I was too afraid to look at him to see his reaction.

"We can't be together. I still love her. I can't stop." His grip tightened, like he was breaking up with me, but not yet willing to let me walk away.

I nodded. It wasn't like I didn't understand. How could he not love her anymore? She was his life. "I know." I stood up and pulled my hand out of his. I felt a chill overwhelm me. It was like his comforting hands had made me feel safe for the first time in my life. I'd never felt anything like that before. "I should probably go."

He stood up and followed me to the door. I could see in his eyes that he was just as confused as me. "I wish it could be different, Vessa."

"Yeah," I cried, "me too."

Once I hit the porch, I never looked back on my way to my car. I don't think that I realized how much I wanted Ramsey Towers—until that happened. It was so intense and I couldn't explain the connection that I felt to him.

It didn't matter though. We couldn't be together for so many reasons.

It just wasn't meant to be.

Chapter 13

Ramsey

It felt like the walls of life were closing in on me. I thought I would be angry for finding out that Vessa knew about my family. Instead, I felt relief. She sat there without judging me and took care of my pathetic ass.

I felt myself more attracted to her than ever before. Of course, this was after I told her that I could never be with her. I stood on the other side of my door, knowing damn well that I only had a matter of seconds to stop her from driving right out of my life for good.

Was I really willing to just let her go?

I thought back to the dream about Jules that had turned to Vessa. The overwhelming guilt was filled with need. Jules was in my head, but Vessa was real. She wanted to touch me. I wondered if she could take away the pain, like Jules had always done.

When I heard the car start, I flung open the door and went running. Vessa turned off her headlights when she saw me coming. She turned off the car and jumped out of it. I could tell that she was both hopeful and confused all at the same time. To explain without using words, I pulled her into my arms and pressed my lips into hers.

Right from the start, our kisses were more intense than the ones from the night before. These were filled with emotion, and for the first time, we both were on the same page. I lifted Vessa up, allowing her to wrap her petite legs around my waist. The palms of my hands were filled with her ass cheeks. I didn't have to assume that my dick was hard as a rock already. That was a given. It had been too damn long since I'd been with someone.

Our kisses became ravenous on our way back inside the house. I used my leg to kick the door closed on account of not being able to stop on our way to my couch. I sat down first, so that she was sitting on top of me. The weight of her body took the wind out of me, at first, when she sat on top of my erection. Her magic tongue licked me, while her sweet lips kissed from one ear to the other. Vessa didn't need to seduce me. I wanted it so badly that my dick was aching to be inside of her.

She rocked her body back and forth, while bending back to enable me enough room to reach under her top. Her skin was warm to touch and it felt so good against my coarse hands. When I got to the underneath of her bra and slipped my hands inside, she let out a giggle. I could tell she was sensitive, so I used more pressure as I moved my fingers up to her smooth nipples.

I couldn't get over how smooth her skin felt and I just had to see what I was touching. Vessa seemed to get shy when I pulled her shirt over her head, revealing her breasts half in and half out of her bra. I reached behind her back and unhooked it, pushing it out of my way. I know it seemed juvenile, but I actually licked my lips when I got my first look at her supple breasts. Her nipples weren't fully erect and I couldn't help but lean in and take them into my mouth, one at a time. She leaned back again; giving me the room I needed to explore every inch of both of her breasts. As I pulled away from one, I left a trail of saliva over the nipple. My lips puckered up and I blew air over it. When her nipple got even harder, she grinded herself into me and moaned.

I looked straight into her eyes. They were full of desire. She teased me with her tongue, not letting me kiss her full on the mouth. I met her tongue in the air and then sucked it into my mouth. Fingernails tickled my sides as Vessa reached down and got ahold of the ends of my shirt. She only had to tug once before I helped her remove it. There was nothing that I wanted more than to be naked and ready for her.

Her cotton pants gave me easy access to be able to slide my hand down into them. When my fingers reached her panties, she took my arm and pushed it the extra couple inches to be touching her sex. I explored her pussy with my fingers by separating her folds and using her wetness to glide inside. If her actions weren't enough to drive me wild, her soaked pussy did me in for sure. I located her tiny bud and rubbed it back and forth. When she began bucking her body into my hand, I knew she was getting off. I kept rubbing at the same pace until she finally relaxed again. I hated pulling my hand out from her pants, but she needed to be naked. I didn't know how much longer I could sit there without coming.

She slid off the couch and got down on her knees. Her hands were on the buttons to my pants and I lifted up so that she could pull everything off. I think Vessa was shocked when she saw me fully erect. Her eyes got big for a second, before she stood up and wiggled out of her pants. Her pussy felt smooth, but to see it all shaved was another thing all together. I reached my hand out and slipped two fingers inside of her folds again. Once I got my finger inside, I used it to pull her closer to me.

"You're so ready for me, aren't you?"

Vessa got this look on her face that seemed almost ornery. "I've never wanted someone this much." She climbed back up onto my lap and let her own juices lubricate the tip of my shaft. If I said that the very first thrust wasn't one of the best feelings of my life, I'd be lying. It took everything I had not to prematurely ejaculate.

I wanted it to last, but was too damn turned on to be in control. The more Vessa moved, the closer I was to finishing. "You have to slow down. I'm never going to be able to pull out in time."

"I can't help it. Kiss me, Ramsey. Please kiss me."

While our tongues began to mingle again, I pulled her ass into each of her thrusts. Her tits bounced up and down with every movement. It forced me to close my eyes, because it turned me on too much. She leaned in closer to me, letting her hard nipples drag over my chest. Her nails ran up and down my sides and then back around my neck. With one arm holding on to my shoulder, she leaned the other back and started riding me like a bull rider.

It was in that instant where I finally lost control. My senses went awry and I was overcome by my explosive release. I held Vessa still until I was able to regain some composure. She giggled and let her head fall onto my chest. Her fingernails tickled my arms as she moved them up and down. I kissed the top of her head and wrapped my arms around her back. I'd prevented myself from experiencing this for too long. Jules would want me to live—I knew she would have. It was just so much easier said then done.

Until the night Vessa came into my life. I didn't believe in fate, but it was a damn strange coincidence that a car accident took away my family and a car accident made me meet Vessa. I knew I could fight my feelings until I was blue in the face. It wouldn't do me any good when the lines had already been crossed. I couldn't fight my feelings for her anymore. She'd put herself out there for me. She'd seen the darkest part of me and didn't run away. I needed her.

About an hour had passed and we were still wrapped in each other's arms on the couch. I shouldn't have been doing it, but my mind did go back to Jules a couple of times. I wasn't sure what was going to happen with my current situation. I wanted to get to know her, but it was impossible for me to let go. As happy as I was lying there with her in my arms, I had to consider how much it would hurt her if I could never move on. It wasn't just Vessa. She came with two kids. It terrified me to think about hurting all of them if I couldn't handle the relationship. Those kids were already hurting from the damage their father had done.

Vessa adjusted her body and I loosened my hold on her. She leaned in to kiss me, but backed away when I didn't respond the way she expected. "Are you okay?"

I ran my hand over her blonde hair. "I think we shouldn't have rushed into this."

She sat straight up and covered her body with her hands. "I thought… we just…"

"I know. I'm trying to wrap my mind around what just happened." Right away, I could tell that it hurt her feelings. She climbed off the couch and started looking for her clothes, before walking into the bathroom and closing the door behind her. I walked up to the door and knocked on it. The sound of sniffles was all I could hear. "Vessa, let me explain."

"I think you said enough. Why didn't you just let me leave? I've never done anything like that before. You're the only man I've been with besides my husband. I feel like you used me."

"You know it's not like that. I told you from the beginning that I was a shitty friend."

The door swung open and Vessa stood there with an angry look on her face. "You didn't have to run out to my car earlier. You can't keep making excuses for your actions, Ramsey. Obviously your dick was ready to be my friend."

It sounded so dirty coming out of her mouth. "Don't talk like that. You know it wasn't like that. I was emotional and let my feelings take over. I never said that I didn't want to be with you. All I'm saying is that I don't know if I'm ready to jump into a relationship with a married woman that has two kids." It came out wrong. I wanted to take it back, but when Vessa went running for the front door for a second time, I just stood there and watched her leave.

Sure, I could have run after her and promised her that things between us would work out, but I'd be lying. My heart was being ripped apart and I couldn't let her in until I knew where I wanted to be. It wasn't fair to either of us. So, instead of running after her, or calling her, I just stood there and watched her drive away.

I didn't sleep at all that night and when morning came, I was determined on what I needed to do. For the longest time, I'd shut out my family because I couldn't face them. I wanted to call and check on Vessa, but the damage was done and giving her false hope wasn't the answer to my problems. She was better off thinking that I didn't want her.

The drive to the cemetery was long and quiet. I stopped by the florist and bought two bouquets of daisies. When I pulled up at the gravesite, I couldn't seem to get out of the car. I eventually had to force myself to do it. Fresh flowers had recently been put on both of my girls' headstones. I knew it was probably my in-laws, since they made it a point to stop by every Sunday after church. I traced Jules' name on the headstone and sat down between the two of them.

I had so much to say to them. It all seemed so easy on my drive there, but sitting in front of those headstones made it all seem real. I felt like I was giving up on them by accepting their deaths. I thought about my sweet little girl and how her hands felt so soft when they held mine. I remember tracing the wrinkles in her skin when she was a baby. I even got choked up thinking about the first time I saw her beautiful smile.

We loved our little girl so much. There wasn't anything in the world that I wouldn't have done for her. I put my flowers in with the other ones and traced Katie's name with my fingers. My eyes burned just thinking about her tiny body being in the ground underneath me. The only good thing was the fact that they were both buried together. I couldn't have them laid to rest apart from each other. They died together and they needed to be laid to rest that way.

My mind went back to that cold winter day the funeral took place on. So many people had come out to support me, but by then, I'd already completely shut down. Not even my parents could make a bit of difference. From the moment of the accident, after I'd looked over and realized that they were gone, nothing could ever be the same for me.

"I miss you so much, my sweet girl. Daddy thinks about you every single second." I didn't care if someone saw me breaking down. This was between me and my girls.

My head leaned down on the large headstone. I didn't know if she could hear me, but I had to talk to my wife. "If your watching over me, you're probably pissed right now. I know you wouldn't want me to live the kind of life that I've been living. I just couldn't stay in that house, Jules. I couldn't be there and not hear you talking to Katie. When I came home from work, the house was too quiet. For the first week, I slept in Katie's room. I didn't know how to live without you two." I'd never been an emotional kind of guy. Some people would have said that I never showed any, but after they died, all of the pain just took over.

"I think I'm here because I'I feel guilty about what I've been doing. Jules, I know I promised to love you forever, and I meant it. I will love you forever. It's just that I don't know if I'm doing the right thing. Someone came into my life and as much as I try to distance myself from her, I can't seem to do it. God, I feel like I cheated on you and I hate myself for it. I just don't know what to do, babe. I need you to tell me. Was it just a coincidence that I met her the same way I lost you? You know I never believed in all this before, but did you send her to me? I get that I haven't been living up to my potential. I just wanted to give up. I wanted to be with you and Katie. Please, Jules, I need you to give me some kind of sign that I'm doing the right thing. I want you to yell at me for sleeping with Vessa. Tell me you're mad. Scream at me. Please! You always used to tell me about signs. You said everything happens for a reason. I need a sign, babe. I need something so bad."

I kept my head against the stone, even after I had run out of things to say. It was quiet and birds were chirping in the trees that were placed around the cemetery. The morning dew had all but dried due to the bright sun having been up for a while. I knew I'd been talking to myself as some kind of therapeutic last resort. Before standing up and leaving, with no more answers than when I had first got there, I needed to say one more thing. "I can't live like this anymore, Jules. I'll never stop loving you and Katie, but if I can't be with you, I need to know if it's okay to live again. I need to know that it's what you'd want for me."

If I tried to tell someone what happened next, they would have never believed it. At the time, I didn't even believe it myself. There wasn't a single cloud in the sky, but it started to rain. I stood up and let it fall all around me. Now, I know it could have just been some kind of fluke weather condition, except I needed a sign and I was too caught up to consider that it could be anything but that.

I was raised Catholic. I'd heard of spirits and exorcisms and miracles. I gave my wife her first cross and had our priest bless it. Was there such thing as divine intervention?

It had to be.

The rain shower disappeared after only a few minutes and the birds went back to chirping. With soaked clothes, I walked back to my truck and got inside. I think I must have sat there for over an hour, shaking at what had just happened. Like I said before, I knew it was probably just my imagination, but it was enough for me to question my actions.

I think all along I knew that the way I was living was only hurting myself. People cope in different ways. I needed time alone. I needed to be able to let go enough to live again.

Now I just needed to figure out how to make things right again. Before I could even consider what my feelings for Vessa were, I needed to do some serious damage control on everything else in my life. It was the only way for me to be sure that I was making the right decision.

Chapter 14

Vessa

After sleeping with Ramsey, and leaving the way I had, I sat in my car crying in my driveway for the longest time. My aunt finally had to come out in her night clothes and get me to come into the house. I think when she saw what kind of condition I was in, she was afraid to ask what happened.

Things got even worse for me the next morning. Apparently, Logan had called his father while the babysitter was watching him. He told him all about Ramsey taking him fishing and getting ice cream. Since I wasn't present during the conversation, I couldn't be sure what all else he had told his father.

When my cell phone rang that morning, I got an earful from Gavin.

Hello?

It didn't take you long to move on, I hear. Did you just think you could replace me with a new daddy for our kids, Vessa? You really think I would be okay with that?

First of all, you need to talk to me, not our son. The sheriff is not my boyfriend and I was never trying to replace you. My aunt asked him to take Logan fishing since you were too busy to do it.

You think I'm going to believe that?

I don't care what you think.

Why was there a babysitter at the house last night? You want to tell me that you weren't with that guy?

I had to work.

Bullshit, Vessa. I called the bar and your aunt asked if I was Ramsey and then said you weren't there. I think you two need to go over your stories a little more if you want people to believe them. Just so we are clear, I've already called my lawyer. She thinks we have a stronger case now that you've also strayed from our marriage.

I never...

Save it. Consider us even. Now the judge can decide who the kids should live with.

You know you don't want them full-time, Gavin. Please don't take them from me. I don't have a boyfriend. Ramsey isn't even my friend. He just lost his wife and daughter in a terrible accident. The man can't even take care of himself. I swear, I'm telling you the truth.

Well, I don't believe you.

When did you get a lawyer?

My parents got her for me. She also said something about getting you for taking our kids out of state.

Gavin, I'm begging you. Please don't do this to me. You know that our kids are my whole world. If you ever loved me at all, if our marriage ever meant anything to you, please don't do this. I was a good wife to you. Please reconsider.

The only way I would reconsider now, is if you moved back home and gave us another chance.

Are you serious right now? You're living with someone that you got pregnant while we were still together.

*How could anything that I've done before compare to that?
How could you really think that I would ever give you
another chance?*

*Keep an eye out for the mail, Vessa. You'll be
getting papers soon.*

I tossed the phone on my bed and curled up in a ball
crying. What had I done to deserve everything that was
happening to me? Asha came walking in the room in her
Sunday school clothes. I heard Logan talking to my aunt
about something.

"Mommy, why are you crying?"

I sat up and hugged her so tight. "I'm just having a
bad day. It just got better seeing your pretty face, though."

"Logan said that Daddy told him we were going to
move home soon. Is that why you're sad?" It broke my
heart hearing her say it.

"Asha, do you like it here?"

She smiled. "I like my room and my new friends.
Aunt Sue always does fun stuff with us and we can play
outside without getting yelled at. I don't want to move back
with Daddy. His new girlfriend is mean and she doesn't like
me."

"As much as I know your daddy loves you, he has a
lot going on right now. A new baby can change things and it
can be overwhelming. I'm glad you like it here. I'd never
want you to be unhappy." I had to really bite my tongue to
say something positive about Gavin. After that phone call I
was ready to drive there and commit murder.

"I wish Grandma could be here, too. She always knew how to make things better."

"She sure did, baby. She sure did."

I tried to spend the rest of the Sunday enjoying being with family. The bar was closed and this was our day to unwind. After getting the kids settled down, I finally sat down on the couch with my aunt and told her everything that had happened between me and Ramsey. She didn't seem shocked about any of it, not even the part where he was so indecisive after we'd slept together.

My self-esteem was already becoming nonexistent, but after Ramsey pretty much rejected me after sex, well, I felt worthless. Maybe my inexperience made him never want to be with me again.

The more I tried to focus on other things, the more I thought about Ramsey and our intimate moments together. His touch was like nothing I had ever experienced before, which of course, made me want to do it again.

Two weeks went by and he never came in to have dinner or shoot pool. I think my aunt felt sorry for me. After years of saying that she wasn't going to let it happen, she started up an in-house pool league so that I could get out and meet people that had the same interests as me.

We had five teams of two people to start out and played what was called scotch doubles. Your turns are alternated as balls are made. It was a bit harder as far as winning, because you had to rely on your teammate to be able to position the ball after they made a shot.

We left the signup papers on the bulletin board for two weeks and my aunt recruited a couple older players that she knew personally. We arranged for the neighbor to watch the kids, so that she could be a member as well. I was having fun and the people were nicer than the ones I had shot with before. My aunt was happy, because it brought more business in. The only thing I was missing was the partner that I wanted to shoot with.

I'd thought about going to see him, but realized that if he wanted to see me, he knew where to find me. Many nights I would cry myself to sleep at what a mess I had made with him. I should have never got involved. It was just that once I did, I couldn't turn away.

Gavin was true to his word. One month after our argument, I was served with papers. I was fine with the divorce part, but him taking the kids was never going to be alright with me. Luckily, my aunt knew someone at church that studied law. He wasn't the sharpest tool in the shed, but he was a nice man who was very devoted to his family.

The battle for custody had begun, and with nothing else to worry about, I focused all of my energy into my kids.

Gavin was trying to prove that I was an unfit parent and that I was out partying instead of being a good parent. The funny part was that was exactly what he was doing, even while we were still together.

So I countersued him.

By that point, Ramsey was just a memory. If someone was watching my every move all they would see was me being a good mom. On the weekends that the kids would visit Gavin, my aunt would drive with me and deal with him so I didn't have to.

It wasn't the kind of situation that I wanted my kids involved in, but none of it was my fault. They were adjusting better than I had expected.

By law we had to be separated for a year before we could file for the full divorce. Since we were fighting for the kids, it wasn't going to be as fast as I wanted it to be.

In the meantime, the kids signed up for sports and scouts. They started having play dates and even Logan loved living in our new town. He especially loved when my aunt brought home a puppy. She was just a mutt, but was the cutest little black and white puppy I'd ever seen. Asha was excited, but Logan had been begging for a dog for years. We named her Priscilla, but we called her Prissy for short. She had longer fur and loved to be brushed and pampered.

Aside from being heartbroken, my life was getting back to the way it was. We had schedules and the children were always my first priority. The day shift gave me more time with them and it also kept me from worrying if Ramsey was going to walk back into my life.

Logan asked about him often but, thankfully, my aunt told him that he moved out of town. I took him fishing a couple times. Of course, he constantly compared me to the sheriff and I couldn't deal with it, so I stopped offering it as something to do on a lazy day.

One morning, after I'd put both kids on the bus, I went into work as usual. The day shift was much different than the evening. A lot of the town frequented for lunch and my aunt had an older man who came in and worked the kitchen for three hours a day. He minded his own business and helped out a bunch.

That particular day, he was carrying in an order of food supplies in the back. I was busy making sure the register was set for the day and packing the deposit for when I got off and dropped it at the bank. To say I wasn't paying attention would have been an understatement.

When someone tapped on my shoulder, from my side of the bar, I screamed out loud before turning to see who it was.

Ramsey just stood there looking at me. I was sure it was him, except he looked different. His face was clean shaven and he wasn't wearing a hat. "I didn't mean to startle you, Vessa."

"What are you doing here?" I didn't say it in a rude way. I really wanted to know why he was standing in front of me.

"I was wondering if I could join the pool league. I have a partner already and we understand that you are already a few weeks in, but we still would like to play." Was he really asking if he could come here to have a good time in front of my face?

"You'll have to ask my aunt. I don't run the league and if it were up to me I would tell you no! I thought you didn't socialize."

"Things change. People change."

"My aunt is at home if you want to call her. She took over the night shift so that I could be with the kids in the afternoons."

"How are things going for you?"

"I thought you didn't care about anything anymore. Do you really want to know about my business?" If he thought that he could come in here and act like we never happened, like I hadn't slept with him, he had another thing coming.

"It doesn't have to be this way between us, Vessa. I never lied to you." He hadn't lied, but he sure didn't have to give me false hope.

"I'm fine about what happened between us. It's water under the bridge. We had a one-night stand. I'll chalk that off my bucket list and move on."

"I'm sorry if I hurt you. The timing was wrong."

I held up my hand to make him stop talking. "I'm a big girl, Ramsey. We slept together once; it isn't like I fell in love with you. Just drop it. You want to come in here and shoot, so be it. I'm just telling you right now that I can't be your friend." Did I just say the "L" word? Had I really let myself fall in love with this broken man?

It killed me to say it out loud and to talk like that night hadn't been one of the best moments I had ever experienced. The whole situation had hurt me when I was already at my lowest point.

"I'm sorry you feel that way, but I understand why you do. I'll call your aunt to make sure it's alright for us to join. Maybe I'll see you around."

When he finally walked out the door, I buried my face in my hands and started to cry. Who was I kidding? My feelings for Ramsey were still there and maybe even stronger from the time that had gone by. I missed seeing him and trying to get the truth out of him. I missed the way he kissed me and how he touched me.

Two nights later, I was sitting with my partner waiting to see if he was going to show up. I couldn't imagine who had offered to be his partner. Since we had five teams before they joined, their team made it even and nobody had to sit out. Unfortunately, the way the schedule fell, I had to shoot him first.

When he came walking in, my heart stopped. Beside him was a tall brunette. Her hair was down her back and she looked like a damn model. She was smiling at something he said.

My eyes met Ramsey's and I knew that he knew I was jealous. He threw me a wink and I rolled my eyes. I wasn't going to let him get to me. I'd tried so hard to be there for him when he pushed everyone else away. Now, he was going out and doing things in public with some beautiful chick at his side?

I grabbed my stick, which had belonged to my father, and headed toward the two of them. My partner hadn't showed yet, so I had to go about things all alone. "We should flip to see who breaks."

Ramsey leaned into the table, so nobody else could hear us. "How long are you going to pretend that the night we spent together didn't change things?"

"Says the guy who came here with another woman and disappeared for weeks, after he told me that he couldn't be with me," I whispered.

"If you'd let me explain then you wouldn't be so mad about it," he said under his breath.

"I'm trying not to think about that night anymore. Can we just play this match before everyone in this place thinks something is going on between us?" I didn't get why he was doing this when he was with someone else. Was he trying to torture me more?

"That would be a bad thing?" When I raised my eyebrow, he shook his head. "Fine, I call tails, because in those jeans all I can think about is the way you looked when you were naked on top of me."

I was shocked that he'd said something like that to me. This couldn't be the same man that I fought to get to know. This man was cocky and sure of himself. I flipped the coin and rolled my eyes. "It's heads. I guess you lose."

"It wouldn't be the first time." He walked back over to his partner and right away I felt jealous. I never met the woman and I already hated her. She was with Ramsey and as much as I was fighting my feelings for him, seeing him brought them all back.

I wanted him.

I wanted to touch him and feel his naked body against mine again.

I was so relieved when my teammate finally came walking over, because I was about to walk over and just put myself out there.

We played our match, but the female and I never spoke. Since it was only one shot partners, Ramsey wouldn't be able to tell my skill level. Luckily my teammate shot better than usual, so he never noticed that I was the higher ranked player.

Still, I couldn't help but notice that he just kept staring at me. I tried to act like it wasn't bothering me, but the truth was, it was driving me crazy. After we played two of our five games, I excused myself to the bathroom. I didn't really have to use the restroom, but I did need to catch my breath. He was making me crazy and I think he knew it. Hell, I think he was doing it on purpose.

When I heard the bathroom door opening, I just figured it was another female coming in to use the facilities. Hands wrapped around my waist and I was instantly spun around to be face to face with Ramsey. "You can't be in here." I never moved away from him.

"I need to talk to you."

"People are waiting for us. You're here with someone." When I said that it made me upset and I pulled away from him.

"If you'd hear me out, I think it would make a world of difference." He was so adamant about me listening to him. I just couldn't deal with hearing that he'd moved on.

"No!"

He grabbed me and pulled me back into his arms. Our faces were only inches apart. I could feel him breathing. His lips were so close. I could feel my eyes starting to close, like I was waiting to accept my kiss. Instead of feeling his lips against mine, he moved his mouth next to my ear. "When you're ready to listen, you know where to find me. I'm not going anywhere."

He left me in that bathroom panting for him. There was no way in hell that I could handle being around him once a week like this. It was going to kill me.

Chapter 15

Ramsey

It had taken me a while to begin to get my shit together. After my visit to the girl's gravesites, I had to face my family that I had shut out of my life. I knew that they were also devastated after the girls died, but I chose to run away rather than face them day in and day out.

Jules' parents weren't that happy to see me again. I had words with her father and made her mother cry. After we all got what we needed to say out, we were able to make amends to the best of our abilities. Since we never got along great, I knew they would never forgive me. It didn't matter. This trip was about being able to forgive myself.

My progress continued to be slow moving until I realized that getting help was the only way I was going to be able to live a real life again. While back in my hometown, I decided to look into grief groups. I went into my first one with sweaty palms and nothing to say and when I came out, I had a group of people who knew exactly what I had been going through.

After a few more meetings, I was able to share my pain openly with others. The urge to drink seemed less necessary as each day I took another step toward moving forward. Being back in my parents' home made it feel like Jules and Katie were all around me. My mother was so happy to see me that she cried every time I was around. I didn't think about how much my leaving had hurt them. They hadn't just lost my girls, they'd lost me too.

After spending a whole week there, and getting as close to my girls as I possibly could, I still couldn't get my mind off Vessa. My late night memories were filled with the night we'd spent at my cabin. I longed to be able to touch her again, even when I knew that each day that passed was probably getting me further and further from that ever happening again.

I'd taken a week of personal time from my job after the whole article about my family came out. It wasn't like the town was burning down with crime sprees. When I came back, people weren't treating me any different. To follow through with moving forward, I found a counselor that I could see once a week, to help me cope with my situation.

Every step I took was to work toward being the man that I once was. I didn't know if I'd ever be able to be with Vessa again, but if I did, I wanted to have my head on my shoulders. With two kids to raise, she didn't deserve to be strung along by someone who was unsure of themselves. As a father, I wouldn't want that myself.

It was tough. I'd make it through the day fine. It was when I went home alone at night that things got tough. I never slept in my bed because it reminded me of Jules and now I couldn't sleep on the couch because it reminded of Vessa. I was running out of places to sleep.

I remembered when I was visiting with my mother, her reaction when I told her about Vessa. I thought she would be disappointed in me; maybe say it was way too soon. Instead all she said was, "Distance makes the heart grow fonder, you know?"

She was right. The longer I was away from Vessa, the more I wanted her. That one night with her had haunted me since she'd walked out of my door.

Call it sneaky, but once I was back in town and seeing a therapist, I had to attempt to get back in Vessa's good graces. I owed my progress to her. She may not have believed it, but it was true. So, I had my deputy stop by the bar to check on her. Shelton loved that I'd finally opened up, so now that we were officially friends, he was all about doing me favors. I was surprised when he came back and said that Vessa wasn't there at night anymore, but they had a running pool league going on. Since pool was something that I'd always loved to do, I decided to find myself a partner and win back the girl. It all seemed easy when I conjured the idea up in my head. Of course, Vessa, being Vessa, the stubborn woman that liked to give me a hard time, wasn't going to be easy to win back. She was going to fight me and I would love every minute of it.

Shelton set me up with his cousin Renee. She was an attractive young woman that was studying law at the university a few towns over. Since she commuted, she said she didn't mind showing up at pool every week. At first I was reluctant about having her by my side when I was trying to get back in Vessa's good graces. It was also a personal test for me, to see if I even still had a chance. The funniest part was that while Vessa was getting all jealous, I'd be laughing inside knowing that Renee was a lesbian and had absolutely no interest in me at all. That's why Shelton set us up.

He knew his plan was going to work.

I will never forget the look on her face when she saw me walking in that door. I winked at her and she curled her lip in disgust. So far it wasn't going how I imagined it. I didn't expect her to drop what she was doing and come running into my arms, but it seemed cool when I played it out in my head. Renee knew what I was up to and she knew that she was basically posing as a decoy. It wasn't like we were going to make out in front of Vessa; I just wanted to get a rouse out of her.

It only took a few games for her to head to the bathroom to pout. She could deny it all she wanted, but that's what she was doing. I found her in there leaning against the sink. Just as I suspected, she denied it and had her normal attitude that drove me wild. If I could have lifted her up to that sink and fucked her right there, I would have. Every single time I looked at her body, I pictured how hot she was naked.

When we both returned to our match, there were a few people giving us looks. Not that I cared. Even Sue's looks didn't bother me. Nothing mattered in that bar except Vessa and she didn't even know it.

Her refusal to speak to me lasted the whole night. Renee was great just being there. While she giggled and talked about things at her school that I had no interest in, Vessa was fuming with jealousy. If she would have given me a damn minute, everything would have been cleared up. The guy she was playing with kept watching her ass every time she bent over for a shot. She was oblivious to his intentions when she probably asked him to be her partner. Why else would someone want to be on her team? The girl sucked at pool, but for what she lacked in billiards skills, she made up in beauty and compassion.

My team ended up winning three out of five games. Since we joined a few weeks behind everyone else, it didn't even matter how we placed. Until I had the partner that I wanted, the league meant nothing to me.

Other teams still had to finish shooting, so I walked Renee out to her car. I didn't want to drive her there in case Vessa did end up running into my arms. Since that plan fell flat, I stayed in my truck and just waited for her to come outside. It didn't take her long and, when I saw her, I took a couple deep breaths and attempted round two of my plan to get her to listen to me. She climbed into her car and I started mine. By the time she turned her body around to back out of the spot, I was parked behind her, blocking her in. I didn't wait for her to come to me. Instead, I jumped out of the truck and went to her. She rolled down the electronic window, but refused to look at me. "What do you want, Ramsey?"

I put my arms on the roof of her car and leaned in the window. "I want to talk to you. If you'd just stop being so damn stubborn and listen to me, we wouldn't be here arguing right now."

"Look, I get it. You needed a push and I was the one to give it to you. I'm happy that things are going better for you."

I was going to have to force her to listen, but people were outside the bar smoking and I didn't want them watching us. "Just forget it!" I walked back to my truck, without explaining, and pulled out of the parking lot in the direction of my house. Once I saw her pull out and head in the other direction, I turned around and followed her.

We reached a patch of woods with nothing around us and I saw my chance. I turned on my police lights and waited for her to pull over. Of course, to make sure she couldn't pull away, I put my truck in front of her car. She put her head on the steering wheel and kept it there even after I got to the window.

I knocked on the glass. She reached over, without looking and rolled it down. "What now?"

"License and registration, please."

Finally, she turned and looked at me. "You can't pull me over. I'm out of your jurisdiction and I wasn't speeding."

"I pulled you over tonight because you have a taillight out, ma'am."

"Screw you!"

"I'm going to need you to step out of the car." I stayed professional.

"I'm going to need you to move your truck and leave me alone."

"Are you refusing to cooperate?" It was so hard not to laugh.

She threw her hands up. "This is ridiculous!"

"Step out of the car!"

I couldn't see because it was so dark, but I knew she was rolling her eyes. She climbed out anyway and slammed the door shut. I got up close to her, pushing her body back against the vehicle. Our lips were almost touching. With the back of my hand, I dragged it up between her legs. "Do you think about that night?"

She moved her head to the side so I couldn't brush my lips against hers. "I try not to."

"Do you ever wonder what would happen if you'd stayed that night?"

"Why are you doing this to me?" It was a plea. She was frustrated, but still not giving in to me. It was risky, but it had to be done. I pulled out the cuffs from my back pocket and got them around one of her wrists, before she even noticed that I had them. "What the hell?"

"Vessa, I'm sorry for what I'm about to do, but you've given me no other options." I secured the other hand and threw her over my shoulder.

She was pounding her cuffed hands against my back. "Put me down! Get off me! I'm going to have you fired, you cock sucker!"

I ignored most of what she was screaming, while getting her fastened into the backseat of my truck. Once I knew she couldn't get out, I grabbed my cell phone and called Sue's bar.

Hey, it's Ramsey. I just want you to know that Vessa is with me and she's safe.

How come she isn't calling me?

She's cuffed in the backseat.

Come again?

She wouldn't listen to me, so I pulled her over and cuffed her. She's too pissed to call you at the moment. I just didn't want you driving by her car and getting worried.

How long are you planning on keeping her?

She'll be in my custody until she hears me out.

Ramsey, don't make me regret pushing the two of you together.

I hung up the phone while she was still threatening me. If my plan backfired, that woman was going to skin me alive.

After grabbing Vessa's purse and pool stick, I locked her doors and headed back to the truck. I should have known she would still be cussing at me.

"Ramsey Towers, you get me out of these cuffs, right now!"

"You have given me no other choice. I'm taking you to my cabin and you're going to listen, whether you want to or not." I adjusted the mirror, to be able to see her while I drove.

She spat out a few other profanities on the way back to my place. I was amused by the way she was acting. In fact, it was turning me on. The angrier she was, the more I wanted to pull the truck over and show her what I wanted.

Once I was parked in front of my place, I proceeded to get her out of the backseat. "If you think you are going to take me in there and have sex with me, you are dead wrong."

She was handcuffed from the front, so it was easy to lift her arms above her head and shove her against my truck. I pressed my body into hers and used my free hand to rub against her jeans, right between the legs. I rubbed her hard, right where her little clit was. She closed her eyes tight, trying to fight what I was making her feel. I put my mouth against her neck. "I bet you taste amazing."

"Please... don't."

I kissed the base of her neck, letting my tongue lead the way to her ear. "Don't what? Don't stop?"

She said nothing.

My hand slid up under her shirt. I could feel the edge of her bra. Instead of going underneath, I stayed on top of the fabric. Her little nipples were hard and I pinched at them one at a time. "You're so damn, sexy. Let me taste you, Vessa."

I stood up and pressed my lips against hers, slowly letting her hands come down over my head. With her arms securely wrapped around my neck, I picked her up. As soon as I felt her legs wrapping around me, I knew we were on the same page. I pressed her body against the truck and teased her with my lips. My dick was already trying to bust out of my pants and we weren't even in the house yet.

I kept a good hold of her while I carried her into my cabin. With my foot, I slammed the door shut. I leaned against it, with her still in my arms, and my hands on her ass. She pulled away from my kiss and looked right at me. "Free my hands."

I kissed her again. "Are you going to smack me?"

"Is that what you want? Are you into that kind of thing? I wouldn't know, since you wouldn't tell me anything." I took the key out of my pocket and uncuffed her. She rubbed her wrist for a second, while keeping her eyes on mine. "Why am I here? You said we couldn't be together."

She backed away from my reach and stood behind the couch. With the furniture between us, I stood up straight and just looked at her. "You're right. I did say that."

She waved her arms around the room. "What is this then? Why did you bring me here? What the hell was the kissing about?"

I pointed to the back room, where a pool table had been covered in storage boxes before. Not only had I cleared it off, but I'd been playing on it every night when I couldn't sleep. I'd even had Shelton over for beers and basketball games. "You wanna go in there?"

"What the... I don't remember this."

"When I originally got this place, it was the only thing I brought from my old house. The place was already fully furnished. Since I never unpacked everything, it was covered up with all my shit." I walked back there and realized she was following me. "The only problem with uncovering it was that I didn't have anyone to play. So, I say we play a couple games. The wager will be what it was before with an addition."

"What if I don't want to know anything else about you?"

"Oh, you do, Vessa. We can keep playing this game if you want, except, I'm tired of wasting time. If you're not naked in my bed before the night ends, then I promise to leave you alone from now on." This was going to be good. I was going to kick her ass on this table. Sure, it needed new rails and the felt was horrible, but she sucked at pool. It was a win-win for me.

She leaned on the table and looked up at me. "What's the other addition?"

"Every time the person wins, they not only get a question, but the loser has to remove one article of clothing."

She cocked an eyebrow and shook her head. When she held out her hand, I didn't quite understand. Then she explained. "Give me your keys."

My plan had backfired. I felt defeated. Why had she kissed me back if she didn't want to be with me? "You're just going to leave me here and go home?"

She didn't answer as she walked right out my door. I should have ran after her, but with everything I had done to get her there, it was too much. While thinking that my chance with Vessa was over, she came walking back in the house and lifted up her pool case into the air. "I shoot better with this."

I didn't want her to see my excitement, so I focused on something else. "I noticed the stick when you were shooting. Where'd you get it?"

"Only the winner gets to ask questions. I think it's time you racked the balls." She pulled out her stick and assembled it together, while I grabbed the pool balls and got them positioned within the triangular-shaped rack. I watched her chalk up the stick and something was different about her.

I was shocked when she broke a ball and made one in the side pocket. From the moment she leaned over, I could see that something was different. She made five balls before hiding me from making my shot. With a huge smile on her face, she backed away from the table.

It had to be luck. I'd seen the girl shoot before and she sucked badly.

I kicked at my shot and missed. Vessa made three more hard ass shots and then called the eight ball in a pocket she'd have to bank it in. I'd like to pass out when I saw her bend down to take that shot and look at me as she did it. That damn ball went right into the pocket. With my mouth hanging open, she looked at me and re-chalked her stick. "Remove one article of clothing. Rack the balls and tell me why the hell you brought me here, for real!"

I pointed to the table. "You… you just… you've been hustling me this whole damn time?"

"You aren't allowed to ask a question until you win. I believe that was the rules that you made."

Holy shit. In all the games that I had played for money, I'd never imagined in a second that she was hustling me. The whole time I was getting to know her, she was losing on purpose, knowing that she wouldn't get one single question. "This is the kind of mind shit your aunt plays," I said as I removed my shirt and tossed it to the side.

She smiled and watched me kneel down and start re-racking the balls. "You owe me an answer."

"Fuck that! I'm going to stand here and be mad at you for a second." I crossed my arms and refused to explain anything to her.

She bent over and broke the balls again, this time making three balls. She ignored me as she made each shot with perfect positioning for the next. I was dumbfounded. "I've been around people with problems for a long time,

Ramsey. I knew you were broken by the second time we met."

"The second time?"

"Yeah, you think I forgot about the hospital?"
Jesus, who was this woman?

"I was making sure you were okay."

"I figured it out when all the pieces started coming together. When the whole truth came out, I really understood why you just couldn't leave until I woke up." I felt like such an ass. She really did know me, even when I tried my hardest for her not to." This time she broke and ran the whole rack out without giving me one single shot. "Second question is why am I here when you have clearly moved on to a very attractive brunette?"

Of course, this made me laugh out loud.

I stepped out of my pants and tossed them over where my shirt was. "Just because I love the fact that this is bothering you so much, I will answer the second question first. Renee is my deputy's relative. She's studying for a law degree and lives right outside of town with her lesbian girlfriend."

Her eyes got huge and I saw the little block of pool chalk being thrown toward my head. "You dick! You picked her to get to me, didn't you?"

I laughed even louder as it passed by me and landed on the floor. "No questions until you win again, remember?"

She shot and missed, *finally*, probably because I had her so worked up. For the next few minutes we played safe on each other, which meant we kept hiding the ball so that we couldn't make our shots. As mad as I should have been, I was hotter for Vessa than ever before. Each time she bent down and stroked her stick with such precision made me want to bend her over that table and rip down those tight jeans she had on.

When she missed her shot, I ran out the rack. Finally having my turn, I watched her removing her jeans, without having to ask. Her tiny little lace panties barely covered her ass. I couldn't help but stare the whole time I asked my question. "What's the real reason you hustled me?"

Her face got red as she stood there in a tight shirt and a pair of panties. I let the question simmer and started shooting. Like a kid at Christmas, when I ran out all of the balls without her having a single shot, I jumped up and down. I got up in her face. "Lose the shirt!"

She leaned her stick up against the wall and pulled off her shirt. Her bra didn't match her panties, but I liked that she hadn't expected any of this. She tried to stand so that her hands covered her body, but I could see through the sheer blue bra. "You owe me an answer, you know."

"You still owe me mine!" I walked up close to her, shocking her when I took one hand and cupped the fabric of her bra. I used my fingers to pull it away from her skin and get a peek at her nipple. I licked my lips before bending down and running my tongue over it in circular motions. Once she was breathing heavy and wanting more, I pulled the fabric back up the way it was supposed to be and backed away from her.

"I think we should play the tie breaker first."

"Fine!" She racked the balls and watched me break the balls. The rack must have been loose, because they didn't break up all the way, leaving a mess to work with on the table. Vessa seemed proud of her little cheat attempt at screwing me over. I shot at a ball and missed the next one.

She walked by me and bent down slowly to take her shot. Before doing it, she turned her head to see me looking at her fine ass. "You should keep your eyes on the table."

"I'd like to put you on the table," I whispered.

She must have heard me, because she missed her shot by a lot. "That wasn't fair."

"Life's not fair, Vessa. You should know that more than anyone. If it was fair, you'd be happy and you're not. There's only one thing that's going to fix your broken heart."

She put her hands on her hips. "Oh yeah, what's that?"

"Me!"

Chapter 16

Vessa

"Did you really just say that to me? You rejected me, remember?" I pointed to the corner pocket and sunk the eight ball. When it rolled in, I tossed my stick on the table and turned around to face him. He walked up closer to me, keeping six inches between us. "You need to start explaining yourself, or I'm going to get a ride home."

He kissed me softly on the cheek and walked over to grab something. Then he walked back and sat it on the pool table. I watched him open it up and stare down at the first set of pictures. "My mother put this together and gave it to me when I finally got the nerve to visit my family again. This is the story of my life with my girls and I want to share it with you and you alone."

I looked down at a picture of a young Ramsey in a football uniform, with a pretty cheerleader at his side. "She wasn't one of those bitchy girls. Jules always got straight "As" and did the right thing. That's what I liked so much about her. She didn't change for anyone."

The next picture was them at prom. Jules looked nothing like me. She had dark hair and huge dimples in both of her cheeks. They looked good together, like the typical jock and cheerleader couple would. I traced the photo with my fingers. "Gavin was my high school boyfriend. None of our pictures turned out like these. He was always too stoned, or skipping school for events like this."

The next set of pictures was their wedding. I looked over at Ramsey and could see from the look on his face that this was hard for him. "It rained that day. I remember the hall we had our reception at smelled like hairspray from all the ladies' hair getting wet. The pictures of our guests were horrible."

We both laughed.

"My wedding was the shotgun kind. My mother didn't like Gavin, so I just did it without her blessing."

More pictures of their life came as we turned the pages together. My heart broke when I saw them at the hospital holding their daughter Katie for the first time. They looked like such a happy family. I could hear him sniffling, but knew I would start crying if I looked up at his face. "She never cried much. We held her all the time. I remember she used to prefer sleeping on my chest to any other place." He pointed to a picture of them both asleep on the couch.

The rest of the album was all the special moments that he'd shared with his girls. "This is beautiful." I turned to look into his tear-filled eyes. "Thank you for showing me this."

He put his hand over mine and took a second to relax enough to talk. "When I lost them, I didn't want to live anymore. I shut down and stayed away from everyone that cared about me. I just couldn't handle the constant reminder of being without them. When I moved here, I just wanted to be left alone. Everything was fine, until I got that call that night. I don't know if it was a sign, but from the first moment I met your family, including your aunt, I've felt connected to you. The more I fought it, the more I thought about you. Vessa, you need to understand that I hadn't let myself live in a long time. I fought it, because I thought you'd be better off not knowing the real me. The one who was broken."

We both turned around and leaned on the pool table, standing next to each other. "It wasn't your decision to make."

"I didn't want to be happy. I wasn't ready to admit that they were never coming back to me."

"I guess I didn't make things easier for you when I was practically throwing myself at you." I just wanted to fix him.

"You didn't have to try hard, Vessa. I was attracted to you from the first moment I saw you. There isn't one thing about you that I would change. Everything is sexy to me."

I looked into his eyes and felt butterflies in my stomach. "You mean—it wasn't because of the kiss?"

"No. I'd been fantasizing about sleeping with you way before that."

I shook my head and looked away. "That's creepy."

He lifted my chin and looked me right in the eyes. "I'm pretty sure the creepy attraction was mutual."

I shrugged. "Even if it was, I need to know what went wrong. I'm listening and I'm ready to hear whatever you have to say. I can handle it, I promise."

"I'll get to that, but I just have to know one thing. Did you only want me because you felt sorry for me?"

That was a hard question. I had to say it right, so that I didn't hurt his feelings. "At first, I was just trying to peel away the layers to what had happened to you. When I found out, I did feel sorry for you, but I was already determined to know you. Learning the truth and how compassionate you were over it is what made me want more. I can't imagine what it was like to live through something like that. All I know is that you did live through it and I hated that you would give up on ever being happy again. I don't know when me helping you changed into something else, but that night we shared together meant more to me than you'll ever understand. I've never been touched like that. I've never felt so connected to another human being than I did in those moments that I was with you. It was when I knew it wasn't just attraction that I was feeling."

He reached over, grabbed my hand, and lifted it to his lips. "I never meant to hurt you that night. What you felt, I felt too. God, I can't even explain it. All I can come close to is that you woke me up and showed me that I could be happy again. I'm so sorry I sent you away, Vessa. I just had all these feelings fighting inside of my head. I didn't know what to do. When you left me that night, I did a lot of thinking about what I wanted. By the next morning, I knew what I had to do."

I let go of his hand. "Obviously, it had nothing to do with me, since it took you so long to walk back into my life."

He slid his body off the pool table and got right in my face. This time, he grabbed both of my hands with his. "That's where you're wrong, Vessa. You're so wrong." He kissed me softly on the lips and pulled away to look at me again. He was smiling and I just wasn't used to seeing him act this way. "I packed my things and went home."

I couldn't believe it. While I was lying in bed crying, he was going out and doing something so brave. I moved my hands from his and wrapped them around his back. My head fell against his chest as I listened to what he was telling me. I felt his arms match mine and we just stood there holding each other.

"The gravesite was the hardest for me. Well, that, and being around my in-laws. They weren't exactly jumping up and down to see me. Anyway, my parents had gone through Hell worrying about me. I should have never shut them out. I get it now."

"So seeing them helped?" I kept my head against his chest, listening to his heart beating.

"Yeah, but the meetings helped me more. I found this group of people that had also lost loved ones. We all had different stories, but shared the same common interest. It helped so much that when I came back to town, I finally broke down and started seeing a therapist. I have a long way to go, but I can already see that I didn't survive that accident to waste my life away. You said that you thought you could help me, but what if we met that night because we were supposed to help each other?"

"With what? I'm doing okay." I didn't need help getting a divorce, that's for sure.

"To love again." The words vibrated off his body. I finally lifted up my head and looked him right in the eyes. "I know you love me, Vessa."

My cheeks were burning red. I couldn't lie about it. I shouldn't have felt that way, but I did and he knew it. "How would you know how I feel?"

He brushed the hair away from my face and kissed my forehead, keeping his lips against my skin. "Because,

I'm in love with you, too." He laughed, but kept his lips on my head. "I wasn't sure at first. I thought it was just my mind playing tricks on me. That's why I pushed you away. I couldn't give you that kind of hope if it wasn't real. After being without you, even the first night, I think I knew it was real. The longer I was away from you, the emptier I felt inside. Then when I saw you for the first time again, I was positive." He kissed me again and then put his hands on either side of my cheeks. Our lips met and I felt his tongue teasing mine. He pulled away, just far enough to stop kissing me and talk. "I knew you were supposed to be with me. Vessa, I don't believe in fate, but I swear you were sent here to be with me."

I started to cry. Never, in a million years, would I have ever expected this to be happening. This intense connection that I felt for him had been mutual. At that moment, nothing else mattered. I grabbed his hair in my hands and pulled him into a deep, sultry kiss. Since we were already almost naked, he picked me up and lifted me up on the pool table. After climbing on top of me, I used my toes to slide down his boxer briefs. He ripped off my bra and had my panties down to my knees before I could offer to help.

Ramsey's hands moved up and down my legs. He massaged each of my thighs while watching himself. I ached for him to touch me in other places, so I touched between my legs myself. He licked his lips and cupped one of my breasts while watching my hand pleasuring myself. He leaned down and kissed my stomach with his tongue. I felt him removing my hand and something warm replaced it. When I held up my head, I saw what it was and almost screamed out in ecstasy. He was kissing me everywhere, using his lips and tongue while exploring the most sensitive part of me. Ramsey kept one hand on my chest. He squeezed my nipples and looked up at me, while his tongue moved up and down my tiny bud. I pictured just what his tongue was doing to me. I closed my eyes and thought about him sucking on my clitoris and when he actually did it, my body tightened and I lost all control of myself. My toes curled and I grabbed a chunk of his hair in my fist. The more I needed him to stop, the more he licked. Rushes of pleasure flowed through every inch of my body. As he kissed his way up my body, I started to shiver. "Kiss me."

I kissed him, tasting myself on his tongue. It made me so hot for him, just knowing how he'd made me feel. My hand reached down and took his hard cock into my grip. His skin was so smooth and I loved the way it felt when I ran my closed hand up and down the shaft. His thickness was exactly the right size to please me, but not hurt. My inexperience seemed irrelevant when it came to being with this man.

He reached over and grabbed the cue ball and ran it from my neck, down to my waist. I watched him smile when he took it and started rubbing it over my wet sex. It was smooth, cold, and the weight of it was enough pressure to have me begging for more. "Don't stop."

He smiled. "I'm just getting started. You like it, don't you?"

"Yes!"

"I've had so much time to think of all the ways I wanted to pleasure you. I couldn't wait to taste your pussy. I dreamed about how good you would taste on my tongue." He removed the ball and licked me with his tongue again. "It's even better."

"Oh, it's happening again!" I screamed out something that I wasn't sure was even English as Ramsey's tongue sent me into euphoria. I bit down on my lip so hard that I drew blood. While trying to catch my breath, Ramsey climbed up and filled his mouth with one of my breasts, while pinching the nipple of the other. My sex was still throbbing as I felt his hard erection rubbing against it. He positioned his body overtop of mine and, without the help of any hands, he slid right in. I was embarrassed about how wet I was, but Ramsey used it to his advantage. He moved so slow, pacing himself, just like he did the first time. Then he took his hand and lifted my arm up into the air. He kissed my tattoos from my wrist to my shoulder. It was so intimate, so intense. People had always judged me because of it and here was this man who loved everything about me.

Once he released my arm, I ran it up and down his chest. He was so sexy. Maybe to some, the tattoos on his arms would have bothered someone. They were special to him and I admired his devotion for his family. It was just another reason that I felt the way I did about him.

Ramsey slowed down even more, trying to make it last longer. Without his suggesting it, I rolled over and sat up. "What the..." He rolled on his back to see where I'd gone. I climbed on top of him before he could finish the sentence.

I straddled his body, only letting my weight on him after he was back inside of me. I leaned down and kissed him, needing to feel that tongue against my own. When I sat back up straight, I hit the pool table light with my head. It felt so good to ride him the way I was that I didn't even care that it was swinging all around. He grabbed my hips and steadied my rapid pace, but I was already determined that I wanted him to feel the same feeling that I'd already had twice. I went faster, letting him play with my breasts while I held my hair up with my hands. It felt so good, grinding against him like I was. I reached up higher and held onto the chain of the pool table light, using it as a push off to grind even harder. The skin-on-skin friction sent me over the edge. I could feel my muscles tightening and I guess he could too. He squeezed both sides of my hips and stopped me from moving. His eyes tightened and his loud groans filled the room. I leaned down and put my lips against his.

He pulled my hair back away from my face with his hands and held it there. "We need to talk."

Before I could tell that it was a joke, he started laughing. I smacked his chest and laughed with him. "I don't know why I'm laughing. That wasn't funny."

"Yeah, it kind of was."

I ran my fingers over his tattoo. "What do we do now?"

"Right now?"

"No! With us. What happens now?" He rubbed my back with his hands.

I leaned on my elbow so I could look at him. "That depends."

"On what?"

"On if you love me or not." He was very direct and since I still wasn't completely used to conversing with him, I had a hard time believing it wasn't a dream.

"You know the answer."

He took my free hand and kissed the back of it. I loved when he did it, so I reacted by smiling. "Do you have something against saying it?"

I shrugged. "No. I'm just scared."

"What are you scared of?"

I immediately started to cry. "I have to tell you something and you're not going to like it."

For as much as I wanted to be with this man, I had to put my children first. Ramsey needed to know what I was about to be up against. "Gavin is suing me for sole custody. He claimed that I was an unfit parent and even said that I was involved with you and neglecting the kids. I have my own lawyer and we are also suing for the same, but it could go either way, especially if…"

"If we're together?"

I looked away from him, unable to face the reaction that I know he was having. "Yes."

He took a deep breath and lifted me off him. I jumped off the table and ran into the bathroom in tears. Unlike the last time, he followed me inside and reached to turn on the shower. "So what if we're together?"

We waited until the water was warm and both climbed in, like we'd done it a million times before. "I'm still married. I'm committing adultery."

"Bullshit! You haven't lived there in months. He's the one that got someone pregnant while you were still together."

"It doesn't matter. Ramsey, if he wins custody, I can't stay here. I have to be close to my kids. I can't lose them." I leaned my head into his chest and he wrapped his arms around me. "I think he hired someone to watch me. I wouldn't care what he thought, except for the fact that it would put me even with him as far as fault goes. If the judge thinks we are both equal, it could go either way. I could lose them, because I'm with you. I can't go to court and have pictures showing up with me having late night embraces with you. He could say I was neglecting the kids to rendezvous with you."

"We're not going to let that happen. I won't let him take them away from you, Vessa. That piece of shit doesn't deserve them."

"So, we're breaking up again?"

He kissed the top of my head and started washing my hair. "Of course not! Look, I know what you're afraid of. You think they'll look into my past and it will hurt you. I'll have you know that with the exception of the past year, I've been nothing but an ideal citizen. My police record is pristine. That's how I landed this position. I spent the last ten years working my way up. We'll just have to be careful. No public affection. No late night meetings. If you come here, you make sure it's dark and you're not followed."

"It's a terrible way to start a relationship."

"Fuck it. Move in with me. I have plenty of room. If you live here, they won't know what happens behind closed doors. This place isn't in my name and my mail goes to a PO Box. The kids can have their own rooms upstairs and if it makes you more comfortable, you can take the room across from mine, until we're ready to make things official."

My mouth dropped open. I think if he wasn't already holding me, I would have passed out. "Did you just?"

"Yeah, I did. I know it's rushing things, but I had to put it out there."

I shook my head. "The kids are just getting adjusted. I can't do that to them. They'll know something is up. Asha is too smart for her own good and Logan can't keep his mouth shut about anything. It won't work."

He grabbed my shoulders and looked at me. "Then we'll have to just play it safe. I'm not going anywhere, not again."

After our shower, he led me to the bedroom. It was a place that he'd held sacred and I wasn't sure how things were going to play out. New blankets were on the bed and the room had a different feel to it. We separated only to climb in and then met in the middle.

Being in his arms made me feel so safe. I wanted this with him, but I had to look out for my kids first. I appreciated that he understood and would do whatever I needed him to do. For this one night, I just wanted to be here with Ramsey. I closed my eyes and focused on his strong arms holding me tight.

Chapter 17

Ramsey

My progress was improving every day, especially knowing that I had a chance with Vessa. Our relationship would have been so much easier if we didn't have to sneak around like teenagers, but it sure did make the spontaneity in the relationship fun.

I had lunch with her most days at the bar. I was in my uniform and the place was packed with other customers. We never touched or acted like we were together when people were around. Some times it was downright hard to not touch her, especially when I knew she wanted me to.

Nights were getting harder to stay apart after about four weeks. Since my truck was easy to spot, Vessa was adamant that we not chance things. The harder we tried to stay away from each other, the more we wanted the opposite.

Gavin had seen the kids several times and never started any trouble when the kids came home. We thought that it was finally safe to slowly bring me around the house again. I was invited to dinner and even picked up some live bait to fish with Logan. My excuse for being there was to replace a faucet in the kitchen. Since they really needed a new one, it was legitimate and couldn't be argued. Just like the last time I was asked to come over for a favor, I brought my tool box and carried it inside. Sue and the kids were in the living room playing a board game. Vessa grabbed me and pulled into the cellar stairway. She kissed me before she even said hello. "I miss you."

"I miss you more."

She pulled me down the steps with her. "I'm supposed to show you where the water shut off is."

Her fingers slid down the front of my pants. She moved her hand up and down, while kissing me again. "How long before they come looking for us?" I asked in between kisses.

She kissed her way down to her knees and yanked down my pants. "Minutes."

In seconds, she had me in her mouth. I let my head fall back against the concrete wall. She worked fast, knowing that any moment little feet could come running down the stairs. Where we were positioned we had time to run, or even hide. I focused on her lips being around my hard cock. She jerked me off with her hands, while her tongue teased my tip. Then she took almost my whole length in her mouth and bobbed her head back and forth. I loved watching her do it.

Since we couldn't be together whenever we wanted, I had to take advantage of the situation. I pulled her up and spun her around, bending her over some storage bins. In one yank, her yoga pants came down far enough. She backed her butt up, eagerly waiting to be filled. I smacked her plump ass, getting off on her giving in to my needs. She giggled and shook her ass again, this time right at the moment I slid inside. We were running out of time. There was no going slow. I grabbed her hips and fucked her hard. She covered her mouth to prevent anyone from hearing us.

I reached around and rubbed hard on her little clit. I could feel her pussy tightening. She was getting off and causing me to do the same. I tightened my hold and filled her with my release. She wiggled that ass one more time before we quickly separated.

I watched her run over with her pants around her ankles to grab a towel out of the dryer. She got herself cleaned up and tossed it to me right as the door creaked open. I pulled up my pants and dashed around the corner. Vessa must have done the same. When I peeked around the corner, she was bent over folding clothes out of the dryer.

"Where is he?" It was Logan.

"I think he's turning off the water, so he doesn't make a mess." I smiled at her quick response.

I came walking out from around the corner wiping off my hands. "Sure is dusty down here. Hey there, Logan. It's been a while, buddy."

"Can I help fix the sink?"

I looked back at Vessa, who was all smiles. "I can't do the job without you."

"Cool! Did you hear that, Mom? I get to help."

He went running upstairs, I guess to tell his sister or aunt. I walked over to Vessa and took her back into my arms. "One day we won't have to hide anymore."

"I love you for having so much patience."

"I love you for loving me." I kissed her nose. She smiled and watched me walk up the stairs.

I didn't mind waiting for Vessa to get her life situated. What killed me was being alone. No matter how happy I was with Vessa, it got hard being alone still. I was trying hard to move forward, but we were at a standstill. It wasn't like I was going to leave her; I just hated this part so much.

Vessa knew how I was feeling. Since we'd been together, for real this time, we promised not to keep any secrets. I was still seeing my therapist and she pushed me to always be open about my feelings. Vessa knew where I wanted her to be. We were so close to being able to make that kind of commitment.

The kitchen faucet was an easy job, especially with a helper like Logan. That kid was pretty damn sharp. I was surprised to find out that he knew the names of his tools. He handed me a wrench and a pair of pliers. In no time at all, we had the new faucet installed. He carried all the old pieces over to the trash and threw them away, while I washed my hands. I was surprised when he walked up and climbed between my arms to wash his hands too. "How come you didn't come back to go fishing?"

I didn't know if this was a conversation I was allowed to talk about. "I'm back now and I brought special bait. Why don't you go ask your mom if we can go?"

She would think it was funny that I was asking, since the last time she'd freaked out so much. She came walking upstairs with a large basket. Instinctively, I took it out of her hands. She got a shocked look on her face. "I could have got that."

"Pretty ladies shouldn't have to carry heavy things, right Logan?" I nudged the kid in his arm.

"Did you just call my mommy pretty?" My smile disappeared. I'd stuck my foot in my mouth, but Vessa was going to stick her foot in my ass if I didn't make it better.

"She's okay. I mean, I bet she looks horrible in the morning when she wakes up."

He laughed. "She looks like a monster." He put his hands up like claws and growled.

"Hey, I'm standing right here, you two."

I grabbed the kid and threw him over my shoulder. He giggled the whole way. "Logan here wants to know if we can go fishing." I gave him a slight wedgie before sitting him back down. He fidgeted with his underwear and then tried to give me one. Vessa covered her mouth as she laughed at us.

"It's fine. Just be back in two hours for dinner."

"Be back from where?" Asha came walking in the kitchen. She gave her brother a dirty look.

"We're doing boy stuff, Asha. You can't come!" Logan did not want his sister going with us.

"I want to go, Mom. That's not fair."

Vessa rolled her eyes and shook her head. I could tell that she thought I couldn't handle them both at the same time.

"Why don't the four of you go? I'll finish dinner. Go have a good time," Sue settled it.

While the girls changed and got shoes on, Logan helped me get the fishing equipment out of the shed. The sun was blazing and it was a perfect day to do this. We walked down to the man-made pond and all got situated on the pier. Logan wanted to bait the worm on all the rods, since he was fascinated that the worm still moved no matter how many times it was stabbed or poked. Vessa was too busy having some girl time with Asha to care what we were doing.

I got Logan situated next to me with his rod. Just like the last time, he swung his legs off the little pier. After making sure the girls had what they needed, I sat back down and cast out my line. At first I didn't notice it, but with little movements, Logan had scooted himself to be right up against me. He leaned his head on my arm and looked up. "Thanks for being my best friend."

I put my arm around the kid and held it there while we fished. When I turned to look at Vessa, she was crying. I smiled and tried not to get emotional myself. I'd never want to replace my family just to move on, but being there on that pier felt so right. I had no problem being a part of these kid's lives, even if it was a small part.

When the sun started to set, we'd caught three fish. The girls caught two, but they let them go, because they were girls and didn't want to touch them. Vessa helped me gather everything up and we walked back toward the shed to put everything away. When my hands were empty, I felt little hands grabbing one. Logan looked up at me and smiled as we started to walk back to the house. Vessa looked over at me and smiled again, while Asha was walking ahead, doing cartwheels in the grass.

Vessa took Logan's other hand and we started swinging him as we walked. He was laughing and having a great time. We all were—until someone cleared their voice and took our special moment from us.

"What's this?" From the amount of tattoos, I took a guess and knew I was looking at Gavin. Vessa turned white as the guy started walking toward us. Logan kept hold of my hand until Gavin crouched down and called him. He kissed him on the top of the head, while looking right at me. "Hey, little dude. Where you been?"

"We went fishing. We caught three fish. Mom threw hers and Asha's back. Ramsey is teaching me how to gut them."

Gavin ignored his son and stood up. He never took his eyes off me. "So you're Ramsey? The same Ramsey that isn't fucking my wife, right?"

"Gavin, stop!" Vessa put her hands over Logan's ears. "Asha, take your brother up to the house to wash up for dinner. Stay there until we get back."

"Is Daddy eating with us?" she asked.

"Please just go to the house, sweetie." I could tell that Vessa was furious. She waited until the kids were far enough away to get up in his shit. "What the hell are you doing here?"

He looked back at me again, like he wasn't afraid that I could beat his little ass. "I could ask you the same thing. I thought you said you weren't with this guy. Then I come to visit my kids and he's holding hands with *my son*." He emphasized the word son.

"I don't have to answer to you anymore. My relationship with Ramsey is none of your damn business. How did you even get my address?"

"It doesn't matter how I got it. I see what's been going on this whole time. Did you meet him online and come here to be together? Is that what you did, Vessa? Did you run right to him?"

I clenched my fists and tried to keep my cool. If he kept running his mouth, this wasn't going to end well.

"I met Ramsey when I moved here. We were friends…"

"Were? So you are fucking my wife?" he asked me directly.

I looked over at Vessa, afraid of doing the wrong thing. Maybe I should have walked away, but his next statement put me over the edge.

"I wanna know if you've been fucking my wife. Are you hard of hearing? Is that how she got you to sleep with her? Are you deaf and dumb?"

I knocked that motherfucker on the ground with one punch. He jumped back up and ran toward me, knocking me down and sending us rolling down the hill. His punches weren't affecting me as much as Vessa trying to pry us apart. Gavin was swinging wildly, trying to make contact with me. When his fist hit Vessa in the shoulder, I lost it. She moved out of the way, holding where he hit her, and I never looked back. I took out all of my anger on him as he screamed and yelled whatever he could in between punches.

Vessa threw herself in front of me, wrapping her body around mine, so that I wouldn't be able to swing without hurting her. "Please stop! Please Ramsey… just calm down. Just calm down."

I wrapped one arm around her, keeping my eyes on Gavin's battered face. "He's not going to talk to you like that, Vessa."

He spit out blood. "Fuck you! I can say whatever I want to her. She's not yours. She never will be. That girl right there has loved me her whole life. You really think you can compare to that?"

Vessa was crying. Her head was against my chest. It was hard, but I managed to stand up and then picked her up off the ground. "You keep thinking that. In the meantime, I'll be the one she comes home to every night. This is the last time you'll ever lay a hand on her."

"Glad you'll be there to pick up the pieces when I take the kids from her. There ain't no judge around that's going to let an alcoholic, worn-out sheriff near my kids."

I couldn't react fast enough to his words. Vessa weaseled out of my arms and went flying over to Gavin, who was just standing up. She pushed him back down on the ground. "I hate you! I hate you so much! Ramsey is a better man than you could ever be."

"Yeah, we'll see if you're still saying that when social services comes for the kids. After they see my face, that verdict will be in my favor."

She went running into the house. As I went to follow her, I felt him grab my arm and yank me back. I fell on my ass and saw him coming at me. My feet lifted and blocked his cheap blow. I rolled and stood up quickly, ready for his next attack. This guy could come at me all night long. He wasn't ever going to be strong enough to take me. "This isn't going to solve anything."

"Says the guy that's been sticking his dick in my wife."

"Where do you get your information from, man? We're just friends. Neither one of us has ever given anyone a reason to think otherwise."

"Let's just say that I know Vessa more than you. She would have come running home by now. I knew she found somebody. I might not have physical proof that you're screwing, but I know you are. I can see it all over her face that she's into you. What's your story anyway? Why do you even want a used-up whore with two kids?" I was going to kill him with my bare hands.

"It's taking everything I have in me not to take four more steps and knock your ass out. I advise you to shut your mouth up about Vessa. You know she's not a whore and a real man doesn't walk away because someone has kids. I don't think you know her at all. You sure as hell don't know me, or anything about me."

We were up in each other's faces again, until Vessa came running down the hill after us again. She pushed us both apart and stood there between us. "Ramsey, go inside!"

"Hell no!"

"The police are on their way. Go in the house. Please!" She was pleading with me, but I wasn't about to leave her alone outside with him.

"I'm not going in that house unless you're with me." She gave me this look, like I was making this harder for her.

"I can handle this. Just go inside and wait for them to get here. I want them to hear the truth before he tells his lies. Everyone knows you acted in self-defense." A smile formed out of the corner of her mouth. She wanted to screw Gavin over and this was a good plan.

Except the police didn't buy it. They took one look at Gavin's face and put me in handcuffs, like I was a danger to be around. I argued with each of the deputies about who I was, but it didn't make a bit of difference. Gavin was pressing charges for assault. I spent the night in jail because I took up for Vessa.

The next morning, when I was released, she picked me up from the police station. I knew she wasn't happy. She looked terrible, like she'd been crying all night long. I ran my hand through her hair, which was in a ponytail. "I'm sorry."

She started talking with her hands, which was never a good sign. "Look, I get that you were taking up for me. I'm not mad about that. He deserved it. What I'm mad about it that you took it to a whole different level after I walked away. The police took pictures of his face, Ramsey. He had to get seventeen stitches in his head and face."

"I... I didn't know."

"What am I supposed to do now? This is exactly what I didn't want to happen. He's going to use this against me. He's going to claim that I put the kids in danger being around you. I'm going to lose them."

I started to answer her when my phone started to ring. I knew it was work related from the number, so I let it go to voicemail. "Vessa, what can I do to make this better? I'm sorry. I just lost it when he got his hands on you. I hated what he was saying. You should never be treated that way. He had no right to…"

"Save it. I can't argue about this right now. I need to do some damage control and you aren't going to like it."

"What's that supposed to mean?"

"We need to be apart for a while. I think if Gavin sees that you're not in the picture, he'll drop the charges."

I wasn't an idiot. "And how are you going to get him to do that, Vessa? You know what, don't even tell me. I don't think I want to know the answer to that."

She slapped me on the chest and pulled the car over to the shoulder. "How dare you think I would do that? I never even considered sleeping with him. Is that what you really think of me?"

"Of course not! I just…"

"I can't do this, Ramsey. It isn't because I don't love you, because you know I do. I just have to protect my kids. You've seen what he's capable of. I wasn't kidding around. He will stop at nothing until he takes them from me. I don't know what else to do." Vessa started crying and there was nothing I could say to make things better. I hadn't slept. I felt like shit and there was no way I was getting out of the assault charges.

I grabbed her hand and pulled her over into my arms. "I am so sorry, Vessa. I just don't want to lose you."

She cried even harder. "I don't either. This hurts so much. I know it's what has to be done. I just don't know how to say goodbye to you, not when I know that you're everything I want."

"I never imagined myself loving someone again. I don't care what we have to do, or how long you make me wait, I'm not giving up on us." My phone started to ring again and it was the same number as before. "I gotta take this. Hang on."

Hello?

Is this Ramsey Towers?

Yes, it is.

This is Mayor Calvin Vance; I think you and I need to have a man-to-man talk about your future in this town.

I can be there in an hour, sir.

My office, one hour. See you there.

"Who was it?" she asked.

"That was the mayor. I think I just lost my job."

Chapter 18

Vessa

I didn't understand how one perfect afternoon could turn into my whole world being turned upside down again. After years of being in a terrible marriage, with the most selfish person in the world, I'd fallen in love with someone that had more compassion than any man I had ever known. Unfortunately, in order to win custody of my kids, I couldn't be with Ramsey.

My heart was ripped apart and I knew his was too. We'd spent so much time building up to, what we thought was going to be, our future. This hurt so much different than being cheated on by Gavin or anything else that we'd been through in our marriage. I guess I never had hope that things were going to last forever with Gavin. Maybe deep down inside, I knew he was going to disappoint me.

At any rate, keeping my distance from Ramsey was tearing me apart.

Fearing that someone could access phone records, he mailed me a pay-as-you-go phone. Our time to talk to each other also got cut in half. Ramsey's meeting with the mayor didn't go as bad as he thought, but he was on probation. He was suspended for a week with no pay, got his second cover story in the local paper, and six months of probation pending the verdict of his trial. Yes, he was actually being sued by my husband.

To say that it didn't cause a major strain in our relationship would have been a lie. Even the kids knew something was going on.

After the whole fight in the backyard, I sat down and talked to the kids about their feelings. They were both very scared and upset at what Ramsey had done to their father. It was hard to explain to a child that their father had instigated it to happen and that Ramsey was only protecting me. Then, of course, they wanted to know why Ramsey was protecting me the way he was.

My aunt was great support, but even she couldn't work miracles.

On one of Gavin's weekends, I decided to take the kids to meet him without my aunt. Ramsey wasn't on board with my decision, but with our relationship consisting of mostly phone conversations, I knew there was little he could do about it. Besides, with his job on the line, he seemed focused on making sure that he was always available for anything that may come up.

Ramsey kept blowing up my phone every five minutes, begging me not go into the lion's den alone. I would be fine. After dealing with this shit for as long as I had, I knew just what had to be done. When we pulled up at the house, all of the memories of the night I left Gavin came rushing back. I don't think that I'd ever felt so angry with someone in my whole life.

The house still looked the same on the outside. Of course, he'd patched up every place that I shot out. The kids ran up to the door, while I took my time, looking around at what was once mine. Gavin came outside when I was walking up the porch steps. He held the door open to let me in.

"Thanks for bringing them all the way here."

I looked right at him and wondered what the hell I ever saw in him. There was nothing appealing about Gavin when I had Ramsey to compare him to. "We need to talk, Gavin."

I walked past him and saw his girlfriend quickly duck into the back bedroom with a baby in her arms. I looked back at Gavin and he scratched his head. "Yeah, she had it a couple weeks ago. I meant to tell you."

I held up my hand. "Just save it. I'm not here to talk about that. I'm here to talk about our kids."

We sat down at the kitchen table facing each other. He reached over to grab my hands, but I pulled away. "I still love you, Vessa."

"How can you even say something like that when the mother of your newborn is right down the hall? Do you even think about the things that you say?" I felt so sorry for that poor girl. She was too young to see that in a few years, she'd be right where I was—raising kids and separated.

"You're my first love."

I raised my eyebrows and shook my head around, covering my face with my hands. "Please stop. I don't care what load of bullshit you want to throw at me. I'm never coming back to you, Gavin. I thought that I loved you and the life that we built, but it turned out to be a lie. The whole damn town knew what you were doing behind my back. How do you think that made me feel?" I put my fist on the table and stood up. Then I started pacing. "I'll tell you how I felt. I felt betrayed. I felt like everything that I'd ever loved was a fucking lie. I felt like the one person that I trusted more than anyone in the world had let me down. It wasn't just me that you betrayed. Those two kids in there, well, you betrayed them too. You broke up this family, not me. I never cheated on you, shit, I never even looked at another man until we were through."

Gavin stood up and walked over to me. He cornered me near the stove in the kitchen. I didn't want to be so close to him. Nowadays, he scared me. I wasn't really certain what he was capable of. "Do you hate me, Vessa?"

I looked him right in the eye. "Yes, I really do." My tears were angry tears. I wasn't crying for being honest with him. I was crying because I'd wasted so many years of my life with the monster standing in front of me. I was crying because he was taking Ramsey away from me. "I wish you could see who I really am. You treated me horribly. Do you even have a clue how hard I worked to save our marriage? All I ever wanted was for you to love only me. I wasn't asking you for much. You stood before our family and God and promised to love only me for the rest of our lives."

Gavin wiped his own tears out of his eyes. He leaned back on the counter next to me. "I will love you forever. I didn't lie."

"You don't know what love is. You think manipulating someone is love? You really think sleeping with other people behind my back was love? You think blackmailing me out of finding real love is the right thing? After everything you've done to me, after claiming you still love me, I have to ask you. Do you love me enough to let me be happy, Gavin?"

He shook his head and sighed. "You can't ask me that. Not after what that dick…"

"Stop! That man that you're talking about lost his wife and daughter. How would you feel if me and the kids died? Would you just go on living normally like we never existed? Could you just forget about us and find replacements?" I walked up close and got up in his face. My heart was beating out of my chest and I was pretty sure that I was about to pass out. "You have no idea what kind of man he is! You have no idea what he's been through. You can accuse me of whatever the hell you want. I don't even care anymore. You and I both know that I haven't been with enough people to be called a whore, so save your pathetic comeback attempts. Stop ruining my life! I know you don't want to raise our kids. You're doing this to get back at me for leaving you, but you can't see that it was exactly what you deserved. I've been the only parent that those kids could count on every minute of every day. You really think they would be happy living without me? You think they will love you more when they found out they can't see me anymore?"

I had to walk away and grab a paper towel to wipe my eyes. While facing the kitchen window and wiping the wetness off my face, I felt his hands reaching around me. I turned around suddenly. "I'm sorry, Vessa. If I can't have you then he won't either. You want me to drop the custody case? All you have to do is leave your boyfriend and move back to this town. You forget all about your life there with him and you can keep the kids without me ever fighting you."

I moved further away from him. "You do know that I can't stand the person you've turned into? You would do all of this to spite me?"

"Yeah, I guess I would."

I slapped him across the face. "How dare you! You selfish son of a bitch!"

He held the side of his face and smiled this arrogant smile, while pointing to the door. "I think you need to leave."

I grabbed my keys off the table and pushed past him. "Gladly!"

"See you in court, bitch!" He slammed the door behind me.

I had planned on staying at a hotel for the night, but after my heated argument with Gavin, I just wanted to go home. Except, that wasn't where I drove to.

When I pulled up at Ramsey's place, all the lights were turned off. It was nearly midnight and I knew that he was probably asleep. Since he was finally able to start sleeping in his bed again, he liked going to bed earlier. I knocked two times before I heard the latch releasing and the door opening. He was wiping his eyes and standing there in just a pair of pajama pants. I threw myself into his chest and started crying.

To be honest, I don't even remember him shutting the door. He pulled me by the hand into his bedroom, where he proceeded to undress me down to my underwear. We said nothing to each other. It wasn't like I could talk anyway, since I was still busy bawling my eyes out. Once he got me tucked into bed, he climbed in the other side and pulled me into his chest. His strong arms held me tight while I continued to let my emotions overwhelm me.

I'm not really sure exactly which one of us fell asleep first. I woke up in a dark room, still in Ramsey's arms. He was snoring, but it was comforting knowing he was there with me. Being there with him, feeling so safe, made me realize just what I was considering giving up. Was

I really willing to let go of this wonderful man, because Gavin wanted to be in control of my life? He wanted me to suffer and I already was. Just imagining never seeing Ramsey again ripped through my heart. I couldn't believe that I had to choose.

I knew what I had to do—what I had to choose—but it didn't make the decision any easier. I started crying again and Ramsey began to stir. He looked over at the clock to see it was three in the morning. "Are you crying again?"

"I didn't mean to wake you up. I'll just go out to the living room." I leaned over and kissed him before getting up. He tried to grab my hand, but I was already standing.

I should have known that he was going to follow me. It was still hard to get used to someone caring so much about me, especially considering the kind of man he was when we first met. He kneeled down in front of me and put his hands on my knees. "Talk to me."

"I can't tell you this. It hurts too much to talk about."

"Whatever it is, we can work through it. I promise you we can." I ran my hand over the whiskers growing on his cheeks. He smiled and kissed my fingers as they passed.

I shook my head and the tears really started coming down again. "I can't tell you this. You're not going to like it. It changes everything."

"I can handle anything, except losing you, Vessa." He used both thumbs to wipe my face and then he kissed me softly. With our foreheads still together, he kissed me once more. "I'm so in love in with you."

His beautiful words ripped through my heart like a sheet of shattered glass. He was everything that I wanted. I could see our future together in my mind. I wanted to be his rock and support him emotionally for the rest of our lives. I hadn't known him my whole life. It wasn't love at first sight. It wasn't even a beautiful love story, but it was our story. All of it brought us to this very moment, where my one decision could make all of our happiness disappear.

I already knew my choice. For me, it was never an option. I think that's why it hurt so much. As a mother, I had to make decisions every day. The most important decision I could ever make for them was to be with them. There was no way I was going to let anyone else raise my children, even if it cost me my own happiness with Ramsey.

"I've never loved someone the way that I love you, Ramsey. You've showed me what it's like to be at the lowest point of your life and find that one light that guides you back to happiness. Now I know that it's possible to be happy after you felt like you've lost all that you were living for. I think that's what makes what I'm about to tell you so hard. It isn't what I would want to choose for myself."

"I'm not following you, Vessa. You're talking weird. What is it? Just tell me."

"I have to leave town." The words almost didn't come out. I found it hard to talk without losing it.

"When will you be back?" He rubbed my shoulders, waiting for me to respond.

I shook my head and looked away from his concerned face. "I'm not coming back. "

"What are you saying? You live here. I live here." I could tell that he was getting worried about what I was telling him. Deep down, I think he knew this was coming. Our struggles to stay together had been weighing on both of us.

This wasn't just about me doing the right thing. His heart was going to be broken, directly because of me. How was I supposed to live with myself? "I'm taking the kids back to the town where their father lives. Gavin said he would drop the custody case."

"I'll come with you. We'll get a nice place and you won't have to struggle. It might take me a while to get into the police department there, but I'm sure I can find something in the meantime. There are plenty of other jobs I can try out."

God, he was willing to move his whole life again just to be with me—to make a life with me. A future. I shook my head again. "You don't understand. If I move back there, you can't come with me."

His eyes got really big. "What do you mean?"

"Gavin will only drop the custody case if I move back home and end my relationship with you."

"I won't let that happen, Vessa. Did you think you could just walk out of my life and it would be okay with me? This isn't okay. I know this isn't what you want." He stood up and started walking around in front of me. I could tell how upset he already was, although, I don't think the whole reality of what was happening had set in. I think he thought we still had a chance, even when I knew that we didn't.

"I can't lose my kids. I don't have a choice. Can't you see that? You think I want to leave you? All I want to do is have a future with you, Ramsey. I've hated having to hide what we have. I want everyone to know how much I love you."

"So, I guess I'm just the bad guy in all of this. I mean, if I hadn't beaten his ass none of this would be happening. Is this some kind of punishment? This is what I get for trying to protect you? I have to lose you now?" His eyes were wet and it made me feel even worse, if that was even possible.

"Please don't make this any harder for me. I feel so horrible already. This isn't easy for me. I don't want to hurt you. You have to know that." I stood up and tried to go to him, but he pulled away from me.

"You don't want to hurt me? You're fucking killing me, Vessa. You're killing me!" He walked back into the bedroom and slammed the door so hard that a duck decoy fell off a shelf. I covered my face and bawled. I moved here to get away from Gavin and he was still ruining my life. Even divorcing him wasn't going to change that.

I didn't know what to do. Ramsey was in the bedroom with a broken heart. I was sitting in the living room, in my underwear, in the same shape. My kids had no idea that any of this was happening. I ran into the bathroom and started projectile vomiting. It was just all too much to take. These were going to be my last moments with Ramsey and I was too sick to my stomach to even talk to him.

Wishing that Gavin got hit by a car seemed wrong in so many ways, but it would solve all of my problems. That's for sure.

It sure beat leaving my heart here and moving to a place where I never wanted to go again.

Chapter 19

Ramsey

I wasn't okay with her decision. There was no way I was just going to let her walk away from what we had, not after everything we'd been through to be together.

I couldn't believe she had showed up in the middle of the night to break up with me. I realized that technically we weren't even supposed to be together, but I wasn't about to let anyone dictate my life, especially when it came to being with Vessa. I wasn't going to let her douche bag ex keep us apart. I didn't know how I was going to do it, but I was going to find a way around this.

When I heard Vessa getting sick in the bathroom, I couldn't just sit around and do nothing. I was hurting, but she was feeling the same thing, maybe even more. I grabbed a small blanket and headed in to check on her.

Her head was lying against the toilet. I wet a rag and handed it to her. "You know, Jules always thought she could drink like her lady friends, but every single party we ever went to, she came home puking her guts up. One time, after a night of puking, she went out and bought me a card, and inside of it, she named me Dr. Pukey, because I knew how to take care of someone else without throwing up myself."

She wiped off her face and flushed the toilet. "You don't have to sit with me. I already know you're my hero. That's why I'm so sick over all of this. It's killing me to walk away from something that feels so right. I never thought that I would ever feel this again. I surely didn't expect for it to happen so soon, but I wouldn't change a thing that got us to this point."

I'd been sitting on the edge of the tub, so she spun around to lay her head between my knees. I ran my hands through her blonde hair. "This can't be the end, Vessa. It's not forever. I'll wait as long as I have to." I just wanted some form of hope. Anything would be better than the feeling that I had in the pit of my stomach when I thought about never being with her again.

"What if he drags this on until they both turn eighteen? I can't ask you to wait that long for me, Ramsey. It's just not fair to either of us."

"So, you're just going to give up? You're going to walk away and not think about me anymore? You think you can really do that?" I clenched my jaw to prevent my emotions from coming out any more than they already were. I knew this was hard for her. "I would never make you choose between me and your kids. I know they are the most important thing. Trust me, I get it."

"Do you? Do you understand that this is only about them?" She was pleading with me to understand. I understood just fine. I just didn't want to accept it.

"Of course. I gotta be honest though. I'm not okay with this decision. I'm not alright with you walking out of my life and I don't know how you're going to go through with it either. Can you really just walk away?"

She shrugged. "I have to."

"I have a better idea. Are you feeling better?" This had to work.

"Not really, why?"

I grabbed her hands and got her standing and then I handed her my toothbrush and kissed the top of her head. "Get cleaned up and meet me at the pool table."

As I was walking out, she sniffled and whined, "Sex isn't going to solve this."

It was funny how she just assumed that the pool table room meant heated sex. "Just hurry up."

I was shooting balls around the table when she finally came in. The color was back in her face, but I could tell that she was far from okay. I mostly knew it because I felt the same way. I made a couple more balls before I could swallow the knot that had formed in my throat. I wasn't going to let her just walk away without a fight. I couldn't give up.

"What are we doing?"

I walked up closed to her and handed her my pool stick, so that I could grab a quarter. I tossed the coin in the air. "Call it."

"Heads."

The coin rolled around the table and finally landed on heads. "Your break, my rack." I bent down and started grabbing the balls to rack them up.

"You want to play a match, right now?"

"Not just a match. I'm playing for your heart. If you win, I let you walk away. I won't fight you."

"And if you win?" She leaned over the table.

I stood up and got the rack straight before looking into her hazel eyes. "If I win, we find another way to be together."

"How is that fair when I want to be with you too?" She had a point.

"If I were you, I'd try to win. You're not going to like what I have in mind." I really didn't have any legitimate ideas. My first thought was to leave town and change all of our names. Maybe I'd watched too many spy movies and it was all just a shitty idea. It seemed better than watching her walk away from me.

"This is ridiculous."

"Just play your game, Vessa. Best out of five. Call your pockets and remember—we're playing for everything. You want me to let you go without a fight, than you're going to have to beat me. I'm just warning you now, when the stakes are high, I don't lose." She was crazy if she thought I was going to fuck this up.

Vessa bent down and broke up the balls. One low ball fell. She walked around the table, like any good player would, to look for her run out. What I was making her play for wasn't exactly right, for several reasons. I wasn't doing this to be mean. I was doing it to see if we had a chance. From the very first shot, I knew this match was going to tell me everything I needed to know. Vessa was just as good a shot as I was, maybe even better. She knew how to play the game and because of that I knew she would play her hardest as long as the stakes were in her favor. If she loved me enough, she'd throw the match. Then I would have my answer.

She made a few balls and then missed a hard cut shot in the side pocket. I could tell from the reaction on her face that she meant to make it. She cursed under her breath and handed me my stick. I walked around the table, deciding what ball I should shoot at first. The trick with playing someone who was as good as Vessa, was to hide her from making a shot if you missed your object ball. It wasn't as simple as running out a rack. It took a lot of thinking.

I started shooting, making one ball at time. After banking two in a row, I felt like I had the game in the bag. That was until she bent over the table, in just her bra, right at the moment that I took my shot. I missed by at least five inches and broke out a group of her balls that were all clustered together. "Shit!"

She grabbed the stick and bent over to take her shot. "What's wrong? Did I distract you?"

"I'll be fine. Next time you try to shark me, don't think I won't put my dick up on this table and fuck you up."

She giggled and made her shot with precise position. Yet another advantage that she had over me was the fact that she could not be distracted. She switched hands and made another ball. "When my dad was teaching me how to play, he used to try and scare me all the time. He said that if I could tune out everything around me, I'd be a better player."

"I wish I got to meet him."

"Eight ball, corner pocket." She bent down and made the shot. "He would have liked you. You're everything that my parents wanted for me. My dad would have given you a run for your money on the table though. He played in a few semi-pro events when I was a little girl."

I started racking the balls, trying not to think about being a game behind her. "Did your mom play?"

She shook her head, but smiled. "No. My mom hated it. I think because my dad loved it so much. He spent a lot of time playing pool, instead of with us. I think she resented the game in general. I know she hated when he taught me how to play."

She broke the balls up and made three. I watched her walk around the table in her bra and underwear. She was so sexy, but with the tattoos and her hair all messed up, she was perfect. Since she got a kick out of distracting me, I walked over and pulled her into my arms, kissing her like we weren't in the middle of a horrible breakup.

Her lips were so soft and puffy. There wasn't anything that I wouldn't have done to be able to kiss them every day. Her tongue always matched my movements, which in turn gave me even more reason to want to kiss her. I pulled away, bringing my mouth up to her ear. "It's taking everything I have in me to not bend you over this table." I cupped one of her breasts and pulled the fabric of her bra down, before sucking her nipple into my mouth. I got it so wet with my saliva that I took my chin and let my scruffy stubble rub it in. She leaned back and closed her eyes. I kissed her little nipple and then between her breast one more time before covering her back up and backing away.

She licked her lips, while opening her eyes. "That's not fair."

"Life's not fair."

She put the stick against the wall and reached behind her back. "You wanna play like that? I can play your game." With one tug, she had her bra off and was swinging it around. I wasn't sure if I should stare at her tits, or close my eyes. She tossed it over towards me and grabbed her stick.

"That's completely changing the rules of the game. I… holy shit that is so hot, Vessa." She bent down and started shooting. The stick, my stick, was brushing against her full breast as she stroked. I bit down on my fist and tried to watch the table and not Vessa. She made it and blew me a kiss as she moved on to the next ball.

When she missed, I knew I had to do something. I held up my finger and ran into my bedroom. In the time it took me to find a clean t-shirt to throw over her head, she'd grabbed my gun holster and my hat, put them both on and was leaning against the table. "It's your shot."

I dropped the shirt on the floor. My hat was too big for her head, but she was hotter than I ever could have imagined. "I'm going to die before I turn thirty." From head to toe, she was perfection. Under my gun holster, which included my gun and clipped on badge, was a little pair of panties. She was barefoot and her tattooed arm was holding the pool stick. I ran into the living room and grabbed my phone.

She covered herself and turned around. "What are you doing?"

"Win or lose, I want to remember this moment for the rest of my life." I didn't think it would change her mind, but she actually turned around and started posing. My dick was so damn hard that my pajama pants felt tight.

When I set my phone down, she put her finger out and motioned for me to come to her. As hot as the gun looked on her, it was the first thing that had to come off. I wasn't about to have my dick shot off, even though I knew the safety was on. She tossed off the hat halfway through my pictures, so all I had to remove was her little panties.

Hard kisses, rough enough to smack our teeth together were followed by her hands discovering just how ready I was to be inside of her. She let out a sound when her hands wrapped around my erection. I picked her up and carried her over, sitting her on the pool table. The balls went rolling all over the table and neither one of us cared about the game or the stakes. I had to have her. She had to be mine.

I ripped off her panties and spread her legs, while tugging my own pants down and letting them fall to my ankles. She wrapped her legs around me as I pulled just her ass off the table. My erection was pressing against her pussy. She was laying on her back with her hair spread all around the table. Pool balls surrounded her body. I licked my lips and watched her touching her breast and rubbing her hands over her smooth skin.

I never thought I'd have this again.

I never knew I would feel this way about anyone again.

With every emotion weighing heavily over my actions, I took my cock and slid inside of her. My hands found her hips and I watched her watching me fuck her. I was so angry, so hurt that I took it out in the way I pounded her. She screamed out. "It hurts... don't stop."

So I didn't. I pumped myself inside of her harder than I ever had before. The more she screamed, the more I thrusted. Sweat started to run down the sides of my face. At the rapid pace I was moving, I wasn't going to last but seconds more. Finally, feeling like I was out of breath, I pulled out of her and flipped her around. Only her ass and legs were hanging off the table. I ran my hands up her back. Hearing her moan only made my dick throb more.

Her ass was so perfect. I ran my hands up and down it, squeezing it. She must have liked it, because she got up on her knees and stuck it right in the air. I ran my hands up the back of Vessa's knees then back up to her ass. My tongue was the first thing to touch her back. I started right above the crack of her ass and licked up to her shoulder. My hands reached around and cupped one of her breasts. I pinched her nipple in between my fingers, while kissing all around the back of her neck.

How could she never want to share this with me again?

By the time I'd made it up to her back, she'd already slouched back down. I'd like to think that I made her weak in the knees. After rubbing my hand all over her ass, I slid two fingers down and separated her warm, wet lips. With her juices all over my fingers, I spread the moisture all the way up to her little asshole. When it nice and wet, I put my dick back up to her sex and slid right in. Then, with one finger, I played with her ass. At first, I just circled around it, but the more she moaned, the more my fingers began to penetrate.

When my one finger slid inside, she screamed out in pleasure. I could feel her pussy tightening. In fact, it tightened so much that she also pushed me out of her. I fought back, thrusting back all the way inside. Her body began to tremble and I just couldn't stop. I turned her back around, so I could see her face when I filled her.

It took only seconds. Once I had a view of her hard nipples bouncing around and leaned down to feel her tongue on my mouth, I pounded my last couple thrusts and exploded my load. She wrapped her legs around me and moved just enough to give me chills all over my body.

I stayed attached to her, while running my hands up and down her naked skin. The sun was starting to come up and I knew where we both needed to be. Without pulling out, I pulled her up and carried her back to bed. She didn't argue or fight with me. When I laid her down in bed, and we finally separated, I felt empty. I'd need more after we rested. Fearing that this could be the end, made me want her on a whole different level. I was desperate to hang on— desperate to experience everything so I had no regrets.

She wrapped her body into mine and laid her head on my chest. I wasn't sure if she was sleeping, but I was wide awake. I thought about losing Jules and what it was like to feel so brutally alone. The emptiness consumed me. I'd avoided people so that I never had to feel that kind of pain again. Now, the one person that freed my lost soul was considering leaving me. I couldn't do it again. I couldn't lose her too.

It would kill me.

Chapter 20

Vessa

Saying goodbye to Ramsey was impossible. I could see the pain in his eyes. I knew the pool game was his last plea. After our game was interrupted and he carried me to bed, I laid in his arms thinking about being without him. More painful than that realization was the fact that I knew he'd never get over it.

He'd given up once from a broken heart, but if I left him, there would be no recovery. Ramsey wasn't about trying all over again. He wouldn't be willing to open his heart in fear of being crushed again. That's not to say that if things were different, and we ended up breaking it off on our terms, that it would be easier for him to move on.

I missed him already and I hadn't even left yet. All of the reasons that I was in love with this man was why it was impossible to just walk away. I don't know how long I laid in that bed before finally falling asleep to exhaustion.

Ramsey's phone woke us both up. He shot up out of bed and went running to answer it. I walked over to his dresser and pulled out a t-shirt. Under it was a photo in a frame. He was holding Katie in his lap and Jules had her arms around the front of him. I traced their silhouette and thought about his painful life again.

Maybe I never should have gotten involved with Ramsey. Nothing in my life had ever ended happy. How could I have thought that he would be any different?

Ramsey came in the room rubbing his temples. He stood there, completely naked, and just stared. "What is it?"

"Where's your phone?"

I shrugged and thought about the last time I had it. "In my car. Why?"

"Sue's had a stroke, Vessa. We need to get to the hospital."

I just sat there, frozen in place. This couldn't be happening, not on top of everything else.

"Vessa, honey, we need to go."

He already had a pair of jeans on. While he was waiting for me to respond, he grabbed a t-shirt and put a hat on backwards. It made him look younger and nothing like he looked in his police uniform. I realized that I was still sitting there in shock. I stood up and ran out of the room to find the rest of my clothes.

By the time we made it to the truck, I was already crying again. Ramsey was pulling down the dirt road before I had the door shut. He reached over and held my hand, but said nothing. I knew his issue with death and how it was for him to be doing this for me.

"Who called you?"

"The station." He turned on his police sirens and started passing a group of cars. "I guess after they couldn't get a hold of you, they called me. Before you moved here, I reckon I was the only person she counted on."

It was amazing how my aunt knew Ramsey was a good person, even when she knew nothing about him at all.

"How bad is it?"

He shook his head and focused on the road. "I don't know. Shelton called and said that they called looking for me, saying it was an emergency. She told them I was her nephew, so I guess when we get in there, we need to pretend we're a couple or they won't let me back with you. Just say I'm your husband."

I looked down at Ramsey's hand that was holding mine. He squeezed it, letting me know I wasn't alone. "I wish you were." It just came out.

"What did you say?"

I laughed and shook my head, turning to look out the window. "Nothing. Never mind."

We pulled into the hospital and the conversation was saved, thankfully. He was at my side when I climbed out of my car and took my hand to lead me inside. After waiting for what seemed like forever, we finally found someone to help us locate my aunt.

They sat us down in a waiting room and told us they would be right back.

I think I knew even before I saw the doctor come in. I wasn't lucky enough in life to have good news. He came out with her chart and sat down in front of us.

His words penetrated through whatever heart I had left.

"You're aunt has suffered a severe stroke. Her left side is unresponsive as of this moment. We're running more tests now, but what has me more concerned is what we discovered already through other tests. Are you familiar with your aunt's past medical history?"

"No."

"Well, your aunt has some serious conditions that may have been the cause of the stroke. Her liver isn't functioning normally and the emphysema seems to be spreading at a rapid rate."

Ramsey put his arm around me. I wanted to throw up, even though I knew I had nothing in my body. "What are you saying? Will she recover?"

"I'm afraid she's missed her window to be treated. I'm not saying that it's going to happen today, but you need to start making arrangements for hospice care. If there's more family you need to contact, I would do it as soon as possible."

I just lost it. Ramsey held me so tight while I just let it all out. We sat in that room until I calmed down enough to go in and see her. I'd just been with the woman only a day ago and she looked so different. Her body seemed weak and it wasn't just all of the machines around her. She looked like a different person.

I saw her open her eyes. One side of her face was completely sagging. It was hard to not cry with her looking at me. She raised the one hand on her functional side. I rushed over and grabbed her hand. She squeezed it the best she could. I could hear her trying to talk to me, but she couldn't say words. When she saw Ramsey walk in the room, she pointed to him. He smiled and came up behind me. My aunt took my hand and sat it down and reached for his. She guided his hand and put it on top of mine. We looked at each other and then back at her.

She focused and tried to get the word out several times, before finally one word came out clear. "Stay."

Ramsey put his other arm around me. "I won't let her go anywhere, Sue. I promise I'll keep her safe."

She patted our hands again. I wondered if she knew her fate. Was that why she was telling us to stay? Was that her last wish for me?

We stayed with my aunt until visiting hours were over. Both of us were exhausted and there was nothing we could do there except wait. We went home and showered before trying to eat something and sleep, which were both impossible.

Ramsey didn't say much, but once I climbed into his bed and he had me in his arms, I couldn't avoid the silence. "She's all I have left and if I hadn't left Gavin, I wouldn't have even been here."

"Someone wise said that things happen for a reason and because of those things you end up where you're supposed to be. I think you were supposed to come here. Look at all the reasons, Vessa. How many more reasons do you need to stay?"

"What if Gavin takes the kids?" I couldn't handle that.

"We'll get them back. Convicted or not, I'm still a better citizen than he is." I sat up and looked confused.

"What do you mean? Why would they compare you to Gavin?"

He smiled and kissed the top of my head. "I heard what you said in the truck, Vessa. Do you really think I'd let you walk out of my life without one last plea?"

I rolled over and acted like I didn't know. Except I did.

He grabbed me and turned me around to look at him. "No matter what happens in that court room, once we're married and situated, no judge is going to give him custody over us." He paused and I could tell the next words were hard for him. "Even if I have to tell them my story about why family means so much to me."

I just stared at him. My world was crumbling and he refused to give up on me. He was willing to risk everything to stay together. I was speechless. "I can't ask you to do that."

"It's my decision to make. Besides, I wouldn't be lying about any of it. After seeing you in nothing but my holster, I'm pretty positive that you're marriage material. At least in every police officer's fantasies."

I knew he was being funny and I appreciated it. I shook my head and lay back down beside him. So much was running through my mind. I wished I could run away from it all. "How am I going to tell the kids? What happens if you actually have to serve time for beating up Gavin? What am I going to do?"

He started laughing. "I won't serve time. I have a good lawyer and he claims he's working on a good case. Stop worrying about what we can't control right now. We need to focus on making your aunt comfortable. It's up to you if you want the kids to be able to say goodbye." He paused again, giving himself a second. "I know it's hard, but at least you have the chance to do it. I know if I had ten more seconds, I could have at least told them how much I loved them."

I kissed him slowly on the lips. "You are such a brave man. Do you have any idea how much I admire your courage? I wish I could have half of what you have."

He sat up, but adjusted so I was still leaning against him. "You make it sound like I did it on my own. You know that isn't how it happened. Without you, I'd still be sitting in the corner of the bar, hiding from life."

My thoughts went back to my aunt and what she did with mine and Ramsey's hands. I thought about my children and how I was going to have to tell them she wasn't going to make it. They needed to be here. They needed to be able to say goodbye. I realized that our conversation was going in all different directions, but I had to focus on my aunt, no matter what was going on with my life. "I want to get the kids tomorrow morning. I'll just drive there and come right back. Do you think you could sit at the hospital and wait for me?"

"No. I'm going with you to pick up the kids. You don't need to be driving when you're so upset. I will take you there and we will get them together."

I wanted him with me, I really did. I just didn't want Gavin getting anymore hairs up his ass. "I can do it. It's fine."

"Vessa, that's it!" He pushed himself off the bed, causing me to fall on my pillow. He paced around the room, saying curse words under his breath. "I'm not going to sit here for another second and let you decide what's best for our future. Damn it, I am driving you there and that mother fucker is going to see my truck in his driveway. He can't control our lives and I'll be damned if he's going to take you away from me."

I leaned up on my elbow, while he went on with his lecture.

"He doesn't make the rules. It's our rules. I know your kids need you, but I need you, Vessa. I need you, too. Stop letting him control you. Be happy, because you can. That life you always wanted. That family. You can have it with me."

I finally got up and stood across the bed from him. "You act like it's just that easy. Like I can just make a decision and everything will fall into place. It doesn't work that way for me. It never has! Please don't fight with me on this. I have too much to worry about." I had to stand my ground. This was about my kids.

"I'm going tomorrow morning, if I have to flatten all your God damn tires, I'm going." He pointed at me and acted like I should be scared.

"Oh, that's real grown up of you to do. Are you going to egg my house next?"

He left me standing there. In ten steps he was walking out of the room and closing the door. I wanted to tell him that he was acting like a child again, but I didn't have time, because he came walking in with a dozen eggs and started throwing them at my shirt. "Oh my God! Stop it!"

I rushed around the bed, to try to get him to stop tossing them at me. He walked right up to me and smashed one on top of my head. I was shocked.

Ramsey backed away and couldn't stop laughing. I put my hands on my hips. "Feel better now?"

He shrugged and kept laughing. "Maybe a little."

I surveyed the mess that was dripping off me. I didn't even know how long those eggs had been in his refrigerator. "Why did you even have these? I know you don't cook."

"I bought them so you could cook me breakfast. You just never have yet. I thought it would be awesome to wake up to eggs and bacon." He laughed even more.

I got why he'd done something so ridiculous. When things got intense, some people shut down. Ramsey used to be one of those people, but he was working to be better. He'd found that using his emotions in a positive way had positive results. Now, I don't think his therapist had this in mind when she discussed it with him, but I did get it.

I dripped slimy egg all the way to the bathroom. While the shower was heating up, Ramsey came in. He started taking off his pajama pants. "What are you doing?"

He walked up and tried to kiss me. I backed away. "Oh no! You can't have a kiss. Not after you egged me."

He laughed again and wiped some of it off my cheek. "But you deserved it." He grabbed the sides of my shirt and lifted it over my head. Slowly, he stuck his fingers in the elastic of my panties and pushed them down my legs. "I love it when you're naked."

"I think you're so tired that you've lost your mind." I climbed into the shower and shut the curtain. He opened up the other end and climbed in anyway. "Seriously? I just want to get washed and go to bed. I have to get up and get the kids. This is serious."

I turned to wash my hair and felt his hands running up the sides of ribs. When he got to my breasts, he didn't stop. His lathered-up hands ran over my nipples. The soapier the suds got, the more he rubbed over them. I leaned my back against his chest and let him kiss my neck. He dragged his teeth over my ear and pulled it gently.

I put my hand over his and let it slide between my legs. He let me control it and where it was touching me. The slipperiness made it even feel better as it slid over my sex for the first couple times. The more he kissed the back of my shoulder, the faster I moved his hand over my wet sex. He was both washing me and pleasing me at the same time. I let go of his hand and let him take over, knowing he was just getting started. "Turn around and look at me."

Slowly, while he held onto my waist, I turned and faced him. Just looking into his dark eyes was enough to make me feel weak in the knees. Ramsey took the back of his hand and ran it over my mouth. When it opened, he leaned in and kissed me, taking his tongue and running it along my lower lip. I closed my eyes and felt him kissing me again. He licked my lips once more, while taking both hands down from my ears to the base of my neck. He grabbed the back of my hair and pulled my head to the side. I could feel his chin sliding up, tickling me.

When he got to my breasts, I was already under his spell. I'd let this man do anything to me. "Watch me," he said before taking my breast and licking the tip. I licked my lips and tried to not close my eyes when he took his tongue and started doing circles around my nipple. He bit it with his teeth and pulled. We may have been in the shower, but it wasn't hot water between my legs that was making me burn for his touch.

"I want you," I whispered, while looking into his eyes. He sucked once more and shook his head.

Ramsey slowly pushed me back against the shower wall. He kissed down to my navel, the whole time massaging my ass with his hands. He grabbed one of my legs and lifted it on the edge of the tub, causing them to spread apart. I heard him growl before his head disappeared between them. Nothing compared to feeling his tongue sliding over my hot sex. I ran one hand through my wet hair and the other I bit down on to prevent myself from screaming out in pleasure.

His fingers entered me. I could feel him spreading my lower lips and licking my entire pussy. His thumb was what kept my clit throbbing, while he continued licking my bare skin. Every time I looked down at him, he was watching me. When my body started to move against his tongue, he used both hands and spread me open more. With only his tongue, he licked over my clit until I finally did scream out.

While still panting, he kissed his way back up to my mouth and kissed me deeply. I wrapped my arms around his neck and let him hold my weight. With his strong arms, he lifted me up and pushed me back against the shower wall. His tongue hadn't gotten tired. No, he kept kissing me, matching my movements. Knowing that his hands were holding me up, I reached down between us and positioned his hard erection at the base of my sex.

The water made his kisses taste sweet. We moved slow, preventing us both from slipping. When it got too hard to maneuver, he carried me all the way back to the bedroom. Avoiding any egg mess that was still on the floor, our wet bodies met in the center of the bed. The second time he entered me felt exactly like the first. Every inch of him filled me and gave me the pleasure that I wanted. Our matched strides increased as our hunger for that blissful release grew. We were both working for the same result. We needed it, after the stress of everything that was standing in our way of happiness.

I sat up and held onto his stomach while riding him. I loved when he reached up and squeezed my nipples at the same time. I rocked harder, knowing that if I came again, so would he. I could feel it growing. That little tickle was increasing. The hot box of ecstasy was opening. I dug my fingers into his chest as I stilled my body for a second and then started rocking again ferociously.

Ramsey couldn't hold it any longer. He closed his eyes tight and held my body so that I couldn't move. I fell down on top of his chest and kissed all over his chin. "You win. You can go with me to pick up the kids."

He laughed. "Yeah, I thought you'd change your mind."

Chapter 21

Ramsey

I didn't know what was going to happen now that Sue only had a short time left. I knew Vessa wasn't going to leave her and it gave me time to convince her to stay. I don't know what I was thinking when I volunteered myself to go with her to get the kids. It was a bad idea.

I knew it.

She knew it.

Except, there was no way she was going alone. To make sure she didn't leave without me, I slept with her body tangled up in mine. There was no way she could crawl out of bed without waking me.

I could tell she was nervous when we got dressed. It didn't help that she had to wear my clothes, which she swam in. "If you had clothes here, you wouldn't have to look like you're homeless."

She tossed her shoe at me. "Shut up!"

I was beyond standing back and letting her make the decision to stay. This was my life too. If I was willing to take her and the kids in, then I wasn't about to let her make the decision to walk away all by herself. I was going to fight for her, whether she liked it or not.

"The only way I'm ever going to get eggs and bacon is if you start staying the night. I'm just saying that it would benefit both of us."

She walked past me and went into the bathroom. I leaned against the door and watched her using my toothbrush. She knew what I was going to say and just shook her head. "Don't even. I have to brush my teeth, you know."

"Yeah, I can see that. What if I don't want to share my toothbrush?"

"What if I don't want to share a bed?" She spit and rinsed the toothbrush before handing it to me.

"Oh, I see how you are." She laughed as she exited the bathroom. Once I was finished, I joined her in the living room. We put on our shoes and she tied back her hair. "You ready?"

"I guess. I just want to get back to the hospital."

"Let's hit the road then." She let me hold her hand as we walked to the truck. I don't even think she understood that every minute that I spent with her made me fall more in love. If she left me, I don't think my heart would survive. This wouldn't be like losing Katie and Jules. No, Vessa would still be out there somewhere, living her life like I never existed.

Okay, maybe she wouldn't just forget me, but it would still be the same to me.

I wanted to be the one to take her pain away. She was the reason I changed. She brought me back to life. I owed her everything. Vessa gave me a purpose. She made me love again.

Losing. Her. Could. Not. Happen.

We set out on our morning venture to pick up the kids. I couldn't help but start teasing her, even though I knew how serious the topic was. "So, maybe I should have brought older clothes in case Gavin wants to go for round two."

Her eyes were wide when she turned and looked at me. I loved that she took me so serious. She was finally getting to know the old me. "So help me God, Ramsey."

I patted her leg. "Calm down. I won't leave any noticeable marks. This time I'm going for bones."

She slapped me. "Would you please stop? I'm so nervous that I need a valium." I should have brought her a paper bag to hyperventilate in. "Or a shot. Although, I don't know of any liquor store that's open at seven in the morning." She wasn't getting a shot, or a valium. Everything was going to fine. She needed to relax and I needed to shut my mouth.

"So, what kind of wedding do you want?"

She put her hands over her face and shook her head, sighing loudly. "Oh my God. I am still married. Do you really want to talk about this?"

I held my hands up. "What? It's a long ride."

"Well, my only family is in the hospital and my best friend is you, so that's my list. I know what you're doing. Stop making me crazy!"

"My parents are going to love you."

Vessa brought her legs up to her chest and hid her face. "I give up."

I reached over and rubbed her back. "I'm sorry. I'll stop," I said as I laughed again.

"They are going to look at my arm and shun me." She didn't realize that she was saying we were going to be together.

"Nah, they'll just say shit behind your back."

She pushed me again. "What is with you today? You're like a comedian or something."

"I guess I'm just happy. I know you aren't used to it. It's probably all these antidepressants I've been taking."

"What? You're taking medicine? Is that why you haven't been drinking?"

We didn't have time for it, but I pulled the truck over. "Seriously, Vessa, I can see why you keep your hair blonde. I'm not on any medicine. My doctor prescribed it, but I haven't felt like I needed it. Well, the other night I could have used some, but other than that, nothing. As far as my drinking, I guess I did that to drown the pain. With you by my side, each day hurts less than the one before it. No bullshit either. I mean that."

"Please stop putting me on this pedestal. I've never been anything to be proud of. You act like I'm some saint. I hustled you in pool to try to get to know you. I let you think I was your wife, just so I could kiss you. Your job is in danger because of me."

"Indirectly!"

"Whatever!"

"We shouldn't be bickering. It always ends the same." I raised my eyebrows and got back on the road.

After driving a ways, she sat up and started giving me directions. As we pulled onto the street, I could tell she was getting nervous. "Ramsey, promise me that you won't fight with him. You're still on probation and this could hurt your trial. You probably shouldn't even be near each other."

I grabbed her hand and squeezed it. "Chill out. We're going to get the kids and leave. No big deal."

I would have liked for things to go smoothly.

They didn't.

When I pulled up into the driveway, it was full of cars. Vessa looked over at me and shrugged. It was still morning, so it wasn't likely to be a gathering or party. "Does he have roommates now?"

"Not that I know of. I was just here the other day." We both got out of the car. She gave me a look but I followed behind her anyway.

When we got close to the door, we could hear yelling. Vessa didn't waste any time knocking. We stood there waiting and nobody came to the door. She ran down the steps and pulled me with her. "Where are we going?"

"To look for my kids."

I didn't understand until she climbed on the air-conditioning unit and looked in a window. I saw her waving and soon Asha was at the window. She was crying.

I stepped in front of Vessa and I held out my hands. She ran away and came back with a baby and Logan. I grabbed the baby and handed it to Vessa, while lifting her two out, one at a time. The screaming was getting louder and, with someone's baby, we couldn't exactly drive away.

I pulled out my phone and called the police, then handed her the phone to give the address. We got the kids in the car, including the baby. She was asleep and oblivious to what was going on. When something came flying out the window, I reached for my gun, instinctively. Of course, it wasn't there. It was lying on the floor in the pool table room. I had another gun locked away in the back of the truck, but there wasn't time. The screaming was louder and we could hear things being thrown. Vessa looked petrified. She ducked back in the car and checked on the kids.

I ran up to where the broken window was and put my cell phone down to record it. If that bastard wanted to screw me over, I was going to play my own game.

When I saw Vessa coming toward the window, I yelled at her to get back in the truck. The screaming in the house stopped. All of the sudden the front door flew open. Gavin stood there looking at the both of us. He pointed at me. "What the fuck is he doing here?"

I'd been around enough people to know he was drunk or on something. His eyes could barely stay open. "What's going on in there?" I asked. "Is everything alright?" I didn't want him to know we had the kids.

He started laughing. "Are you for real? Get the fuck off my property, before I claim self-defense again and shoot your ass."

I almost wanted to smile because I was recording him, but I could tell that something else was going on. "Where are the kids?"

"Fuck you, cop. I'm not telling you shit. Get off my property." He could barely stand up.

"Look, I didn't come here to start trouble. Why don't you calm down and tell us what's going on? We only came to pick up the kids. Vessa's aunt is in the hospital." It wasn't his business, but I needed to get in that house. Something wasn't right.

Vessa just stood there looking at him with a shocked look on her face. I couldn't tell what she was thinking, but it couldn't be good. "Hey, get in the car, honey."

Yeah, that was a dick move. I didn't care. He needed to know that she was mine.

"You can just turn around and go home. The kids aren't going anywhere with you. Ask your honey about our agreement." He started laughing and waving his head around. "You can't have her," he sang.

I rolled my eyes, still waiting to hear the police sirens.

Gavin came down two of the three steps on the porch. He looked from me to Vessa and then back to me again. "You want a piece of me, man?"

It would have felt real good to beat his ass again. I shook my head. "Not here for that. Who's in the house, Gavin?"

"Nobody."

I knew he was lying.

I could see someone moving around in the window. "Who's in there?" I called into the window.

"Get away from my house, dude." He took another step and was on the sidewalk.

The sirens were in the distance, but they weren't close enough to help me with this situation. "Where is your girlfriend?"

"She's sleeping." He laughed again.

I looked at Vessa and she returned my concern. "Did you hurt her?" she asked.

He laughed and started walking back in the house. "That little bitch is fine."

I waited for him to get in the house and then I handed Vessa my truck keys. "Take them down the street and stay there until I come for you. No matter what, you promise me that you'll stay there."

She took the keys and nodded. "What are you going to do? He's never acted like this before, I swear." She followed me to the back of my truck. I grabbed the carpet and opened up the hidden panel where my gun and vest were. She pushed the small box out of my hands. "No! You can't!"

I leaned my head in the truck. "Asha, I need you to tell me what is going on in the house, sweetie. Can you tell me what you saw?"

She looked at her mother and then back to me. "They were fighting. She gave me the baby and told us to hide. Some other people came and she never came back in the room again to get us. That's when you came."

"Good girl." I pulled Vessa away from the truck. "You and I both know he has a handgun. Get the kids out of here. The police will be here any second. There could be someone in trouble inside. This is what I'm trained to do. I won't hurt anyone if I don't have to."

She was crying again. I put my vest on and put my gun behind my back. Vessa climbed into the truck and started it. She leaned out the window and let me kiss her. "Please be careful."

"Go."

I imagined Gavin coming out with his gun firing. That's how a cop movie would play out. Instead, it was much like every other domestic situation I dealt with. Until we talked to everyone involved, we had to be prepared for the worst. Whatever came out of the house, I didn't want Vessa or the kids around it.

I put my back up against the house and listened for movement.

I could hear him yelling. "What do you mean the kids are gone? Well, look again. They didn't just run away with a baby."

A couple minutes passed. "Gavin, they aren't in there. We need to get out of here. You know they called the cops. They can't arrest you for anything if we leave." It was a female's voice.

"I can't leave without my kids. Find them!" I heard screaming again. "Tell me where they are! You sent her here, didn't you? I knew you'd fuck this up for me. I never should have fucked you!"

The girl continued to cry.

More muffled sounds were close to the window. I ducked to the side, just in time for him to peek his head out. Without my badge, I could put myself in harm's way. I saw them pulling in and around to the side of the house. I waved down the officers and they came over to meet me.

"My name is Ramsey Towers. I'm a sheriff in West Virginia. Look, my girlfriend and I showed up to pick up her kids this morning. They were hiding in a room, with a baby. We managed to get them out of a window, but…"

"Wait. Are you dating Vessa?"

I shook my head. "Yeah."

"So, Gavin's in there. Is she in there, too?"

"No! She took my police vehicle and got the kids out of here. I was just waiting for you to get here."

"Any idea what's going on?" Since he knew Vessa, he seemed to be comfortable enough to believe that I was a cop.

"I know he's under the influence. I didn't get close enough, but his eyes were messed up. His words are slurred and he seems unstable. I could hear things breaking and a female screaming. Vessa thinks more than one other person is inside based on the vehicles. Also, she said he has a handgun."

They both looked at each other and then back to me. "She should have took it when she shot up the house. He tried to press charges on her, but I kept losing the paperwork. Gavin's an asshole. The best thing Vessa could have done was left. I'm going to call for backup and then we'll go in and figure out what the hell is going on this time."

"This time?"

"We were here last week and last night. All he does is party. He's got that baby in there and I don't think his girlfriend is even twenty-one." He grabbed his radio. "Five one five six, I'm going to need backup at my location. Can you have Officer Tanger respond?"

Once he got confirmation, he put his radio back in place. It beeped again. "Five one five six, please be advised that a report of children missing just came in for your location."

He put the radio back up to his mouth. "Copy that."

I held up my hands. "We didn't kidnap anyone. Vessa's right down the road."

He drew his gun, but walked by me. "Stay here!" I watched him walk to the front door. "Police! Open up!"

The door opened and Gavin came walking out. "What seems to be the problem, Officer Friendly?" He laughed at what he called the guy.

"What's going on, Gavin? We got a call for a noise disturbance. You fighting with your old lady again?" They were talking like they were friends. I didn't like it.

His partner walked up behind him. "You mind if we come in and make sure everything is alright?"

"Yeah, I mind! You got a warrant?"

"We don't need one when we can smell marijuana coming out of your windows." I stood there and watched them handcuff Gavin. It was going to take a lot more than pot to make sure he left us alone.

Another cop showed up and ran in the house. I sat on the curb and watched them put Gavin in the police car. A few minutes later an ambulance arrived. They went running into the house and came out with a female on a stretcher. I ran over to the girl. She was conscious, but had a busted lip and a wrapped-up leg. "Is she going to be alright?"

"She might have a broken leg. He locked her in the closet and knocked her around. She's crying about her baby, but there are no kids in the house."

The other officer came walking over toward us. "I need you to call Vessa and tell her to bring the kids back. We're going to need to interview them and get the baby to her grandparents."

I walked over to the window and grabbed my cell phone from the ledge.

Ramsey? Please tell me you're okay?

I'm fine. The cops need you to bring the kids back. Gavin's in the back of the cop car, so he can't hurt anyone.

I'll be there in two minutes.

As soon as she pulled up, the police crowded around the truck. I think the other cop was shocked when he saw her pull up in my police vehicle. She pushed through the officers and ran into my arms. "I was getting worried."

"I'm fine. They need to interview the kids."

Another female came walking out in cuffs. She looked around as she was pushed in the back of the car. Vessa's cop friend walked up to us. "We got him on possession and assault. I'm hoping his girlfriend's family will convince her to testify."

"Thanks, Tommy." Vessa gave him a hug.

"I thought you told me that you'd never date a cop."

She turned and looked at me. "I might marry one."

Tommy's eyes lit up. "Really? That was fast. I mean, you've only been gone for like a year."

"She's just trying to skip the dating part," I teased.

"Well, congrats. You got a great girl there. Be good to her." He started walking back to his patrol car.

She turned and wrapped her arms around me again. "Are the kids alright?"

"Yeah, they're shaken up. I hate that I have to tell them more bad news. I mean, they just watched their father get arrested. How much more can they take in one day?" She was so stressed and we hadn't even been to the hospital yet.

"The good news is that I recorded him admitting that he set me up and the police have enough on him to make sure that he won't ever be able to take your kids away. I know it's going to be an adjustment for the kids, but I'm not letting you out of my sight. I think we need to sit them down and give them the good and bad. Together, of course." At first, I thought she was going to shoot down my idea. I could only push her so much before she felt smothered. She was depressed and I was ecstatic. I'd felt so damn guilty about putting her in danger of losing her children.

"Together sounds like a plan. After all of this, I'm just so glad that you were here with me. Can you imagine how bad it could have gotten?"

I kissed her on the top of the head. "Get in the truck. I'll give them all my information to get in touch with you, if they need it. We need to get these kids to the hospital before visiting hours are over."

When I opened my door to get in, Logan climbed over the seat and hugged the back of my neck. "Thanks for rescuing us. You're the best hero, ever!"

Chapter 22

Vessa

The kids didn't say much on the way home. I could tell that they were completely freaked out. About halfway down the road, we stopped to eat. Asha needed to go the bathroom, so I took her while Ramsey and Logan ordered our food.

When we got into the ladies' room, she hugged me. "Please don't make us go back there again."

I held her close and then kneeled down to be on her level. "What happened, honey?"

"Daddy got so mad. He kept yelling. Grandmom came to get us and he fought with her. She said she was going to call you and he told her that she would never see us again if she did. I just wanted to go home."

"You're safe now, baby."

"Is Ramsey your boyfriend again?" I had to laugh at the way she asked.

"Yes, he is. Is it okay?"

She nodded and smiled. "Yes. I like it when you're happy."

"Oh, baby, I like being happy too. I'm so glad you're okay with him being around. I didn't want you hating me. I know you love your daddy. Ramsey would never try to take that from you. He just wants to be with us."

"Aunt Sue said that he used to be sad all the time too."

I wiped her face with a paper towel. "He was. One day he will tell you all about it. It's his story to tell though, okay?"

She nodded. "Okay."

When we went out to join the boys, they were playing with onion rings. "Look Mom, we have new glasses," Ramsey said as they both had onion rings around their eyes.

"Do you know how greasy your faces are going to be?"

They laughed and started eating their onion spectacles. "Everything okay?" Ramsey asked.

I grabbed his knee under the table. "I think it's going to be."

He leaned over and kissed the side of my head in front of the kids. Logan started laughing and Asha's eyes got huge. Logan tossed an onion ring at him. "You just kissed my mom."

Ramsey tossed it back. "You're right, buddy, I did. You want to know why I did it?"

My stomach knotted up. This was not a calm confession.

"Why?"

He leaned in and looked at both of the kids, with onion rings around his eyes, of course. "Because I love her."

Logan covered his mouth with his hands and his little eyes doubled in size. Even Asha was smiling.

When I looked over at Ramsey, he winked at me. "Guess we don't need to finish that game."

I popped a fry in my mouth. "Oh, we're going to finish it; the stakes will just have to be raised."

"Woman, I will play you any day."

The kids giggled more as they finished their food. Ramsey got a kick out of being around Logan and acting silly, so of course, Logan thought he was the coolest thing ever. I thought Asha was going to be a problem. If her father wouldn't have dug his own hole, she probably would have been upset about me being with another man.

Gavin had caused me so many problems. I still found it hard to believe that everything was going to work out perfectly, only because it never had for me before. I just wanted to be able to breathe. With the traumatic events of earlier in the day, I knew that telling the kids about my aunt was going to be devastating. The problem was that it couldn't wait. She was running out of time.

I felt like my life was spinning out of control and at some point it was going to crash. Ramsey seemed sure of his intentions to be with me, but if he lost his job, I wasn't sure how much of the blame would be on my shoulders.

Instead of telling the kids that Aunt Sue was running out of time, I just told them that she'd gotten sick and we needed to visit her. I didn't think about how scary it would be for them when they went into the room and saw her hooked up to so many machines. I could tell she was happy to see them, but it was sad to see her struggling. Plus, her one side was still sagging and Logan was scared to get close to her.

She seemed happy and the nurse told us that she wasn't in any pain. Ramsey sat in the chair with Logan. They found something on the television that had them both occupied. Asha stood next to my aunt and held her hand. They'd really gotten close since we moved in. She was like a grandmother to them.

When visiting hours were over, I knew I had to get the kids home. They had school in the morning and needed baths and a good night's sleep. I also had to call their teachers and let them know what they'd been through. I had a feeling that it was going to cause problems for them. Children were resilient, but this was a little more than us rolling around in the backyard and the police showing up.

We all kissed my aunt and headed back to her house. Ramsey wanted me to just get clothes and come to his house, but the kids needed some kind of stability after going through so much in one day. I just didn't see it going over well.

Ramsey dropped us off at home and left to go get clothes. In the meantime, I made sure the kids had their baths and a snack. By the time he returned, they were both ready for bed. He came in when I was tucking in Logan. "Everybody alright in here?"

"Mommy, can Ramsey sleep in my room?"

I laughed, but Ramsey walked over and plopped down on his twin-sized bed. "It's all good. I think some buddy time is a great idea."

Immediately, they started talking about something that was clearly a topic they had discussed before about some super hero. I stood in the hallway, listening to them getting to know each other. As much as I loved the idea of them bonding, I had this feeling in the pit of stomach that something terrible was going to happen. What if the kids actually fell in love with Ramsey and he realized that he couldn't be in a family environment?

It could happen.

They would be heartbroken.

So would I.

Suddenly, even with everything else on my plate, my optimism went out the door. I didn't know what to do. My children were always going to be my first priority. Since we'd moved here, Ramsey had slowly come into the picture. It wasn't like he just showed up one day and we were together. The kids knew we were friends. They were the ones to tell their father about us. That was months ago and Ramsey was a different person.

Maybe that was what had me worried.

Clearly, he'd made progress with being able to live again. I was so proud of him, even aside from me being his so-called reason for change. Still, that was going to wear off. I wasn't always going to be the only woman that he noticed. I may have been the first one to push him to live again, but I was certain that I wasn't going to be the only woman to come onto him.

He wasn't even thirty and was already the sheriff of a small town. He was beyond good looking and his newfound sense of humor was more than sexy. Every woman would want him and for the first time in his adult life, he could be a bachelor.

I'd lived in a marriage with broken promises. I wasn't naïve. I knew that it was easy to tell someone one thing and want another. How was I supposed to be sure that I was making the right decision? This man had been a challenge and ended up stealing my heart. He'd taken my worries away from my failed marriage and occupied my curiosity enough to move on. I owed him just as much as he owed me.

Losing him wouldn't just crush me. It would crush my kids and they were already losing everything they ever loved. Was I really going to be selfish and put my needs in front of them?

What if his undying love for his first wife started to get to me? How could I ever compete with a love like that?

By the time I climbed into bed, I was in tears. I laid there thinking about everything. I wondered if my leaving had turned Gavin into such a monster. He wasn't ever violent like that with me. A baby wasn't going to know its father now. The mother was going to have to do it all alone. I knew that their circumstance had nothing to do with me. The police would have eventually come back to that house. Gavin had made his bed and the wrong choices and so had his mother for not telling me what was going on. She knew that wasn't an environment for them to be in and she left them there anyway.

Then there was my aunt. My poor aunt, who had lived the last few years of her life alone. I felt so guilty for that. My mother would have been so disappointed in me for not keeping in touch with her. I loved her so much and I owed her everything. She'd taken us in when we had nowhere else to go. She fed us and gave me a job. She started a new life for us. Now she was dying and somehow her last wish was for me and Ramsey to be together.

The stress of it all was making me queasy again. I ran to the bathroom and threw up my whole dinner.

I heard footsteps walking on the porcelain tile and then saw extra large feet beside me. The sink turned on and a cold rag wiped my head. "Thank you," I whispered.

"You okay?" He sat on the edge of the tub, just like the last time.

"It's just stress. I feel so sick to my stomach. All these thoughts keep clouding my mind. I'm worried about the kids and how all of this is going to affect them. I want them to be able to get through it, but they can't handle it all at the same time. I don't even know what's going to happen with Gavin. I mean, how am I supposed to trust him to see them again?" I leaned back against the tile wall.

He reached over and grabbed my hand. "You're not alone, you know." He pulled me up and kissed the top of my head. "When you feel better, I'll be in your bed." He started walking out of the bathroom and turned around. "Oh, and don't worry. I'll go down to the couch before the kids wake up."

I wanted to tell him about my worries, but I was so afraid he would get mad and leave. I just needed him so much.

Ramsey was under the covers when I came in from getting a quick shower. One of his arms was behind his head. His chest was bare and I liked the way it looked to see him there. He cleared his throat when I came in. I loved how fast his facial hair grew, and since he hadn't had time to shave, it almost looked like he was growing a beard. Plus it was a shade darker than the hair on top of his head.

Since the kids were in the house, I chose to put on a pair of pajamas. I could tell from the look on his face that he was disappointed. "You know I have to wear clothes. What if they walk in?"

He lifted the covers to show me that he had on pajama pants. "This isn't my first rodeo, Vessa."

I climbed in next to him, wearing a tank top and pajama pants. I tied my hair back in a ponytail that was on my nightstand and cuddled up against him. "I know."

"Everything is going to be alright. This is just another bump in the road."

"I know. It just hurts so much." I was trying so hard not to start crying again.

"It does." He rubbed my back and didn't say anything else.

I sat up and looked him right in the eyes. "I love you."

"I love you." Ramsey took his finger and pulled down one of the straps to my top. "I don't think you even understand how much."

Hearing the words gave me chills. It was comforting and made me want to thank him. I slowly moved on top of him, straddling his body as I sat up. I slid down the other strap to my tank top and pushed it down over my breasts. Ramsey wasted no time pulling me down to his chest. His kissed me slowly and I matched his technique.

He kissed my nose. "You're so beautiful."

My body warmed up, hearing him say those words and look at me the way he was. I kissed his neck and ran my tongue up to his ear. After nibbling on his ear, he started moving his hands up the back of my tank. I started moving my body, taking my hand and reaching it down his pants. I whispered in his ear, "Make love to me," and he obliged.

Ramsey rolled me over and ran his hand over my cheek as he placed gentle, soft kisses over my lips. He was technically on top of me, but keeping his weight off my body. He ran one hand between my exposed breasts and sat up enough to watch himself doing it. The way he looked at me made me feel like I was being devoured, sexually and emotionally. I could sense his intentions in the way he paced himself, circling one of my nipples with his fingertips. "I love your breasts." He leaned down and kissed my nipple. Then he sat back up and used the palm of his hand to get it as hard as possible. "I love how your body responds to my touch."

I could feel myself catching fire between my legs. My sex was aching for his attention. "I want you so bad," I cried.

He kissed me again, letting his tongue drag over my bottom lip. He slid his hand down my pajama pants. Even I could feel how ready I was for him. "Mmm, you don't waste any time." I could feel him sliding his fingers between my folds and feeling how ready I was for what was coming next.

Except, that wasn't what was coming next. Ramsey pulled his hand out and sucked on his fingers. It was so erotic. "You taste so good." With that, he slid down, pulling my pants down with him. First he rubbed me, while watching both my face and what he was doing. He licked his lips a couple times while sliding a finger inside of me. Slowly, he moved it in and out, using his thumb to rub my throbbing bud. I ran my hand through his disheveled hair. He reached for my arm, sliding his other hand into mine. Our fingers locked around one another. It was such an intimate move.

He kissed my inner thigh, using his tongue as a guide, making his way to my sex. I felt his finger being removed. He adjusted his position and kissed the base of my pussy. I sat up, feeling the need to watch his every move. He kissed it again, keeping his eyes locked on mine. When I felt his tongue sliding in between my folds, I couldn't help but close my eyes for a second. I forced myself to watch him pleasuring me. This wasn't like the last time. He moved slowly, kissing me with every lick of his tongue, like he was savoring me.

I ran my hands up my abdomen and my breasts. I was so turned on by his passion. His focus went to my most sensitive spot. As his tongue made contact with my clitoris, I could already feel my body beginning to shake. The harder his tongue pressed against it, the more my body began to jerk. I grabbed his hair again, making a fist within it as he brought me to bliss. Even after he knew what he'd done, he continued licking it, forcing the extension of yet another bout of euphoria. My head fell back against the pillow due to my losing control of all of my senses.

I felt Ramsey kissing his way back up my body. I was still trembling every time his lips made contact with my skin. He wiped off his face with the sheet before kissing me. I could still taste myself and I think he knew it. He groaned when our tongues met.

When I tried to flip myself on top of him, he stopped me, shaking his head. "You asked me to make love to you, Vessa. That's what I'm doing. Please let me please you."

I fell back down on the pillow, unable to control every emotion I was feeling for him. He slid his body and teased my entrance with his hard erection. As it slid over my swollen bud, I wanted to scream. I was still hot for more, waiting to be filled with his love. When he started to penetrate me, I took a deep breath and focused on every inch of him being inside of me. He moved slowly, savoring the way it felt as it moved in and out.

He looked down, in between us, and watched himself moving. I saw him biting his lip and concentrating on my body. Then he dropped back down and kissed me passionately, while taking my hands and lifting them both above my head and interlocking his into mine. I don't know what it was, but it was the most intense sexual experience that I'd ever felt.

We were connected, in every way possible. His intentions were motivated by his love for me. I felt overwhelmed again, but this time it was pure ecstasy. I clenched both of his hands and let go of all the pain. At the same time, I felt him tightening up. I wrapped my legs into his, locking us together, and he just froze.

When I opened my eyes, I knew something was wrong. He was breathing heavily and I knew that he had finished, so I couldn't imagine what had happened. He let go of my hands and reached down to my legs, pulling them off his. Then he sat up and let his feet fall off the edge of the bed. I sat up and wrapped my arms around the front of him, kissing his shoulder. "What's wrong?"

He sort of laughed and shook his head. "After our first time, when I disappeared, I spent time at the cemetery."

I leaned my head on his back. "You told me."

"I felt like I cheated on her, Vessa. It wasn't fair to you if I couldn't move on. I just needed to know it was real."

I was starting to get scared. "What are you saying?"

"You may not believe this, but I begged her for a sign. I begged her to let me know that it was okay to love again and it started to rain. There wasn't a cloud in the damn sky and it rained. I know it seems stupid, but I felt like it was her. Then after all that time being away from you, and after we got together, it just felt so right. It felt like I had loved you forever. I didn't know if it was because I just longed to feel that again, or it was something else. After you said you might have to leave me, I'd made my mind up that I wanted to do whatever I had to do to keep you. Even with all of the shit that's happening, all of the things trying to stand in our way, there's no place that I'd rather be."

I climbed off the bed and kneeled between his legs. "Then why are you upset?"

He pulled my hair out of my ponytail and smiled. "I guess I just wasn't prepared for what just happened."

"I felt it too. I've never felt a connection like that."

He leaned over and kissed the top of my head. "It wasn't just that. Every time we've been together, I get lost in you. Please don't take this the wrong way, because I'm not thinking of it the way that you're going to think I am. When I was with Jules, she used to do this thing. I'd never had it happen before."

I closed my eyes and looked away, trying to bite my tongue. "The thing with my legs?"

"It's not what you're thinking." He was trying to assure me.

"What then? I feel like you're comparing me."

He smiled, grabbed my hands, and kissed them at the same time. "That connection that we were both feeling, well, it was so intense. When you did that thing with your legs, it was just another sign for me. It didn't make me think about being with her, Vessa. It freaked me out because I know without a doubt that this is exactly where I'm supposed to be. I feel like you know me better than I know myself. How is it even possible to feel like I've always loved you? I'll never forget my girls. A part of me will always love them, but this connection goes way beyond anything I've ever had. Do you feel it too? Am I crazy? I mean, I've lost my mind before. I gave up on life and shit. It's possible I am crazy."

I looked up at him and saw the intent in his eyes. I appreciated that he was so honest. I ran my hand across his face. "No. You're not crazy. You're amazing." I ran my fingers down his muscular arms. "You're brave and strong. You keep me safe and want to take care of me. It was never hard for me to love you, even when I didn't even know that's what it was."

"So, just to be clear… you're not leaving, right?"

I shook my head.

"And, you don't care who tries to tear us apart?"

I shook my head again.

"And, you definitely want to be with me?"

This time I shook my head and leaned in to kiss him. "Definitely!"

Chapter 23

Ramsey

I'd found my place again, thanks to Vessa. The next few weeks weren't easy, but I stayed by her side the whole time. It took her a week to tell the kids that their dear aunt wasn't coming home. Asha, being the oldest, took it harder than Logan. He still believed that super heroes were real and heaven was a place you could visit on weekends.

Sue passed away on a Monday. She ended up getting pneumonia and couldn't fight anymore. We'd had her moved to hospice and kept her as comfortable as possible. The place was less scary and the kids came every day after school. Vessa kept the bar closed and postponed our pool league due to what was going on.

I think we were both surprised at the amount of people that came out to pay their respects at the funeral. That day was especially hard for me. After I lost my girls, I swore I never wanted to attend a funeral again. Just knowing how much Vessa needed me changed all of that. I stood by her side, even when she broke down completely. Watching her was like seeing myself all over again. I had to force her to eat. I stayed at the house and fed the kids, microwave dinners and pizza, since I couldn't cook at all.

For two days after we laid her aunt to rest, she stayed in bed. She needed time, but we needed her. On the third morning, I was determined to get her out of bed. I picked her up and carried her into the bathroom, sticking her directly under a running shower. She screamed and fought me, but I kept her in there. Then, as she began to cry, she rushed over to the toilet and started getting sick.

My clothes were soaked from dealing with her. I grabbed us both a towel and covered her up. "You sure this is just depression?"

She shrugged. "What else could it be? Nothing hurts but my stomach. I just feel so tired from everything."

I stopped trying to dry myself off and looked right at her. "I just remembered that I have to run into town to my office. Are you going to try to get up, because the kids can't survive on what I've been feeding them?"

She actually laughed and stood up. I kissed her and saw myself out.

My ride into town was filled with anxiety. I couldn't believe that she didn't think about it. I needed to know. If there was even a slight chance for it to be possible, I just had to know immediately.

I got weird looks at the pharmacy when I bought the test. Everyone knew who I was. They were going to talk and I finally didn't give a shit what they said. I smiled as I handed the cashier the money and nodded to everyone standing around with their mouths open.

It was time for everyone to know about my secret relationship.

It was a good thing that Sue had planned ahead and had a will drawn up. Since Vessa was her only living relative, she left the house and everything in it to her. Vessa now had her own house to raise her kids. What shocked us both was when that lawyer named who she left the bar to. She didn't just leave it to her niece. My name was listed as co-owner.

We were both shocked at first. She'd had the will drawn up a month before Vessa moved in with her. It was when I was just someone she saw a few times a week and knew nothing about. If so many things hadn't happened to me personally, I never would have believed in fate. Vessa and I were meant to meet. If it hadn't been for that accident, I would have met her later anyway.

I kept teasing her about how she would have hustled me out of my ownership. I could see her playing me for the deed and pretending she couldn't play, then coming back and taking me for everything. If anyone in the world was going to hustle me, I wanted it to be Vessa. That woman had my permission to do whatever she wanted with me.

I got back to the house about an hour later. Vessa was in the kitchen, doing the dishes. She was wearing a pair of my pajama pants and a little t-shirt. I could tell that she got back in the shower, because I could smell her shampoo when I walked into the room. She smiled when I came in, like she had been doing every day since we made the decision for me to move in.

It was the kid's idea at first. They said they were scared. Then it just seemed like the right thing to do. I was still moving my things over. Most of the furniture wasn't mine. I had my deputy help me bring over the pool table first. Logan and I had been spending a lot of time cleaning up the basement. It was going to be our man cave.

Vessa put the rag down and walked over to me. "What's in the bag?"

I smiled and put it behind my back. "Promise you're not going to get mad?"

She rolled her eyes and reached around to grab it. "Just let me see."

I handed her the brown paper bag and stood there watching her face as she pulled out the little white box. She sat it on the table and looked up at me. "You're crazy. I'm not pregnant."

I slid it closer to her again. "Appease me. Take one of the tests. Prove me wrong."

She stood up and grabbed it with an attitude. "Fine, but I think I would know my own body."

I followed behind her, eager to see the result, even if my gut feeling was wrong.

She opened everything up, sat down on the toilet, and started laughing. "I can't pee if you're watching me."

I turned around. "Sorry."

"Or standing there!"

"Damn, Vessa, I'll wait outside." I only waited until I heard the toilet flush before walking back in the bathroom.

The little stick was sitting on the sink. I grabbed it and ran into the bedroom, locking her out. She ran after me, beating on the door. "Let me in! You're being ridiculous. It's not going to be positive."

I put the stick on the dresser and stared at it. I didn't buy one of those cheap ones with lines or crosses. This one said pregnant or not pregnant. The directions called for three minutes, but in less than thirty seconds, I had my answer.

I just stood there, wondering if I was disappointed or relieved. Vessa already had two kids and after losing Katie, she and I hadn't even talked about having kids. I looked at the stick one more time before taking a deep breath and unlocking the door. She held out her hand and I placed the stick in it. "Here! Know it all!"

She rolled her eyes and smiled until she looked down at the stick and saw that she was wrong.

"Say something."

She looked up at me and was already crying. "Is this okay?"

I pulled her into my arms. "It's better than okay, Vessa."

"Really?" She seemed unsure, like I was just saying it to make her feel better.

"When can we tell the kids?" I wanted to tell everyone. I wanted to call that damn newspaper and tell them.

"After I see a doctor."

I couldn't help it. I pulled her into my arms and started to cry. She held me tight, knowing what I was thinking about. I'd never want to replace Katie, but I loved being a father and having a baby with Vessa brought the whole family together.

I didn't care what anyone said. This was where I was meant to be. Even for a person who never believed it, I knew it had to have been some kind of divine intervention.

We waited three weeks to be able to tell the kids about our news. Vessa was so nervous, but I assured her that we all needed some good news. We took them out to dinner to the fanciest place in the area.

They got dressed up in church clothes and knew something special was happening. Vessa ordered them both t-shirts. One said "I'm the big brother" and the other said "I'm the big sister." We let them open each of their packages and figure it out themselves. Of course, Asha got it right away. "Mommy, really?"

Vessa grabbed her daughter by the hand. "Are you upset?"

She shook her head. "No way. Can I help out?"

"Of course. I'm going to need help."

Poor Logan was still staring at the shirt. "It says that you're going to be a big brother." They already had a little sister, but since they never saw her, we figured they would get what the shirts meant. Still, Logan just looked confused. "Buddy, your mom is going to have a baby."

"Do you get to be the dad?"

"If it's okay with you." I realized that I probably shouldn't have offered a child a chance to decline.

"Will it be a boy? Will Mommy get fat? My teacher is fat—is she having a baby?"

We all started laughing. "Whatever it is, we're going to love it."

I think Vessa finally started to relax after the kids were on board. The old farm house that we lived in had plenty of rooms in it, especially once I was allowed to officially share a room with Vessa. We took things slow, never taking the kids' feelings for granted. I didn't mind as long as they were all happy.

Since Vessa was pregnant, it was important for me to make sure she had the proper medical care and insurance. In order to do that, she had to be married to me. Once their separation wait time was met, she filed the papers for divorce.

With all the trouble he was already in, Gavin didn't fight her on it. He probably would have if he knew she was carrying my child, but it wasn't his business. In some ways, I almost wanted to thank him for treating her so terribly that she had to leave him. It was what led her right to me and I was grateful.

We didn't do anything fancy to get married. After we had our license, we went up to the court house and did it. Later that day, we were at the bar, painting, like it was just a normal evening.

After much consideration about the future of the business, we had decided to convert the bar to a family restaurant with a lounge and billiard area. My job was pretty easy. As long as I had my phone and my truck, I could be anywhere and respond to a call. Since construction was so expensive, we did all the work ourselves. Vessa could only help when it was safe for the baby. I wouldn't let her carry anything or paint if there was going to be fumes.

We didn't have a mortgage on either of the properties, so most of our income was put into savings. It was funny how I had worked so hard before to make ends meet and now we had more than either of us could ever ask for.

I was going to continue working as a sheriff until I could retire. Vessa would run the restaurant and we would hire people so that we could spend time being a family.

After several postponements, due to Gavin's other legal matters, the charges against me were dropped. It seemed that after hearing Gavin on my recording, confessing to everything, his lawyer didn't want to represent him anymore. I think it made it worse that I was in law enforcement myself.

His girlfriend never did testify against him, but it didn't matter. The drug charges were enough for a judge to never allow him to take the kids from us. Vessa wanted him to still see them. It just wasn't going to happen until he got help.

The kids talked to him on the phone and even the computer, so it wasn't like they lost him in their lives. He just had to be straight first, before Vessa was going to give him another chance.

I loved her being pregnant. Not only was she beautiful, but it bonded us closer together. One Sunday, after church, I took the kids outside and told them what happened to my first family. They were sad. I could tell it affected them, seeing me get emotional as I told my story and talked about Katie. I showed them a picture of the three of us and Logan grabbed it and disappeared in the house.

At first I thought the worst. We went into the kitchen to check the trash first. Then we saw him walking out of the living room. "I put them where they go."

Vessa looked worried. I crouched down. "Where's that, buddy?"

He grabbed my hand and pulled me into the living room, then pointed to the mantle. Next to all of our new and old pictures was the picture of me and the girls. I couldn't hold back my emotions that day. That boy, who was already so special to me, had added my girls to the people he considered family. It wasn't just special for me to see them up there. It made it all real. They weren't ever going to let me forget them. They'd be there every day with me. Logan went running back outside to play with his sister.

Vessa grabbed my hand as I stood there looking at that picture. "I've wanted to put that picture up there for weeks, but I was too afraid to ask. I can't believe he did that."

"It's perfect. Thank you so much." I kissed my beautiful wife and put my hand on her stomach. "For showing me how to love again and giving me a second chance to do it."

"I got something out of it too, you know." She kissed me softly, letting her puffy lips linger on mine.

I took her by the hand and led her down the stairs. Mine and Logan's man cave was coming along. We had sports memorabilia on the walls, a flat-screen television and I'd even got him his own pool stick. I handed Vessa a stick and started racking the balls. She chalked the tip and blew on it. "What are we playing for, Mr. Towers?"

"Well, Mrs. Towers. If you win, you get to pick the name. If I win, I get to pick it."

She smiled and bent over to break up the balls. "This is going to be easy."

"How do you know I wasn't hustling you all this time?" I laughed just saying it.

She made two balls and walked around the table. It was funny. I was so used to seeing her play in tight jeans, or nothing at all. Now she wore a maternity sundress and had bare feet, but she never looked more beautiful to me.

"Does it really matter? I think we both came out winning."

I watched her shoot at another ball and make the shot. "Yeah, we sure did."

She missed her shot and walked over to me. "Here's your chance, hustler."

I smiled and thought back to when I was playing her to stay with me. "I think you like letting me win."

She started laughing and shook her head. "Only when it gets me what I want."

I bent over to shoot and looked up at her. "So, do you have what you want?"

She leaned against the table, letting me look down her shirt. "I have more than I could have ever hoped for."

I missed the damn shot because I was too busy peeking at her tits. She stood up and started laughing. "You need to work on being distracted."

"You need to wear hoodies when we play."

She reached back and unzipped her dress, letting it fall to the floor. "Oops!"

"I forfeit." It took me only seconds to make it around to where she was standing. "You don't play fair."

"I play to win," she said as our lips brushed.

We heard the kitchen door slamming and two kids arguing. Vessa reached down and grabbed her dress, while I headed for the steps. "Cheaters never win, you know," I teased.

"I love it when you're losing."

"I love it when you're naked!" I laughed as I ran up the last couple steps. I knew she was playing games with me and I loved every second of it. We both loved the game of pool. It had brought us together. She was the only partner that I needed. One day I would beat her fair and square. I had our whole lives to do it.

Chapter 24

Vessa

Our story was far from being romantic. Some may have said that we rushed into it. Others have said that it was a relationship based on two people rebounding.

We didn't care.

Our love was real and we were happy.

I didn't meet Ramsey's parents until I was seven months along and already his wife. He'd talked to them frequently, but we just never had time to take a trip to visit. I would have been nervous meeting them as his girlfriend, but meeting them after we'd already married and gotten pregnant wasn't exactly reassuring. I was so nervous that I threw up the whole way. The kids were excited, realizing that new grandparents meant more Christmas and birthday presents. My husband was the only one who remained calm, smiling the whole way.

We pulled into a small community with only a few houses. Each one looked different and they were surrounded by large pine trees giving each yard complete privacy. His parent's house was a large, white colonial. It sat off the road and had a long, circular driveway. Black shutters were dressed around every window and it was fully landscaped.

I felt like it was more from a movie than an actual place that Ramsey had grown up in. "Don't let the size fool you. My dad built it and they got the property for next to nothing. It's the idiots that have moved into the neighborhood after them that are the rich ones."

I tried to smile, but still felt overwhelmed. It wasn't just that I was meeting his parents. I felt like I had to compete with Jules. I felt like they were going to look at me like I was just a replacement. Maybe it was selfish, or possibly my hormones. Ramsey always said I was the only person who thought things like that. He said that Jules and I were very different and he loved me because of that reason.

At any rate, by the time we got to the front door, I was shaking like a leaf. The kids were giddy and standing behind us talking about being at a mansion. It wasn't close to being a mansion, but I guess it was the biggest house they'd been in.

When he took my hand and opened the front door, I thought he was going to have to carry me in. My feet wouldn't work. He leaned down and started laughing at me. "Seriously, you act like they're horrible people. Would you just calm down?"

Reluctantly, I squeezed his hand and proceeded into the foyer. We found his parents sitting in a family room off the kitchen. His mother stood up and came rushing over toward us. After hugging her son, she turned all of her attention to me. She grabbed both of my hands and gave me a once over. "I am so happy to finally have you here, Vessa. Talking to you on the phone and seeing pictures just doesn't even compare to spending time together. You must be exhausted from your long ride. Come sit down and I will get you something to drink."

"Thank you." Ramsey smiled as his mother pulled me into the living room. His father stopped us before I could sit down. He reached his hand out to shake mine, but I hugged him instead. He seemed to get a kick out of it. I noticed that on his arms he had a couple of old military tattoos. I'd worn a cardigan to try to hide what was on my arm. I had no idea what these people would think of me and I wanted to make a good impression. I didn't have any family, so having them was special.

For the next few hours, I got to know the people that raised Ramsey. His mother broke out photo albums and told stories of when he was a teen. She talked about Jules, but not in a way that made me feel uncomfortable. She even talked about Katie, not that she had to. Her walls were covered in her.

For dinner, his mother, Maggie, made a turkey and we ate a feast like it was Thanksgiving. We joked about how Ramsey couldn't even boil water without burning the house down. He was trying to do better, since we had a restaurant to run.

Ramsey's father, Joseph, took the kids on a nature walk and told Logan all about being in the war and what it was like to be a soldier. They talked about planes and then they got to talking about fishing. Asha followed Maggie around like she was her apprentice. I enjoyed seeing her bonding with another female and it seemed like Maggie felt the same way.

Throughout the day and into the evening, Ramsey kept making sure that I was alright. When it was time to go to sleep, he climbed into bed humming. It was strange to hear, since he'd never done it before. "My parents love you. I told you it would be fine."

"They're really nice people. I told your mom that they need to come stay with us when the baby is born. The guest room will be ready by then." Right now it was full of all of Ramsey's things from the cabin.

He placed his hand on top of my belly. It was something that he did every night. The closer I got to our due date, the more I knew that he was becoming anxious. I knew what he feared, and although I couldn't predict the future, I was certain that everyone was going to be okay.

Sometimes our life together seemed surreal. I had never imagined being so happy with someone. He loved the kids and they loved him back. He was good for them, always making sure they were never left out, especially when it came to decisions about their baby brother or sister.

Finding out the sex of the baby had been a huge ordeal. Since I was still young and had never had complications with my first two, our insurance only covered two sonograms. We had one at twenty weeks and that poor technician tried her hardest, but couldn't get a good enough look to make a determination. So we'd been suffering to know ever since.

Ramsey swore it was going to be a boy. Since I already had one of each, it didn't matter what I had. My main concern was that it came out healthy.

"My dad wanted to know if you'd be interested in…" Ramsey stopped mid-sentence.

I leaned up and looked over at him. "What's wrong, honey?" He just seemed off.

"They have the cradle that he made for Katie up in their attic. He asked me tonight if I wanted it for the baby."

"What did you tell him?" I could see it in his eyes that he didn't like talking about it.

"I didn't say anything. I couldn't talk about it."

I reached out and rubbed his back. "I think it would be really special if the baby got to use the same cradle as one of its big sisters."

He pulled my hand up to his lips and kissed my wedding ring. The diamond was my mother's and it meant so much to be able to finally wear it. "How do you do that?"

"Do what?"

"Always know what to say? Where would I even be without you?"

I tried not think about that. Our life was too great to think about what could have been. "It doesn't matter. You're always going to have me. I can't get rid of you now. I have three kids to raise," I teased.

"We have three kids to raise. As my best friend and my wife, I'll never let you do it all alone. That goes for Asha and Logan too. I know they have their dad, especially when he gets his shit straight, but I want them to know they can always count on me." He laid his head down on my stomach and, after a few seconds, the baby started moving around. "I'll miss them everyday, but this is exactly where I'm supposed to be."

I felt his hand reaching into my panties. "Are you seriously trying to get freaky with me in your parents' house?"

He laughed and kept moving down lower. "Maybe."

I grabbed his arm, not letting him go any further. "We can't!"

He sat up and pulled out of my hold, then started pulling my panties down. "We can! This was my room. I think it's like a fantasy to sleep with a woman that's even sexier than the ones that used to hang on these very walls."

"I am fat and pregnant."

"You're beautiful. I want you every time I look at you."

I rolled my eyes. "Seriously, buttering me up isn't going to make me want to have sex."

He tugged one last time, getting my underwear completely off. He was ignoring me, pulling off his pants anyway. He grabbed one of my legs and held it up against his shoulder. His gentle, wet kisses covered my ankles, leaving me fighting to hold my ground. Once his lips got to my calf, I was pretty much forfeiting the battle.

Ramsey had a way of persuading me into doing whatever he wanted. He was never really unreasonable, so I went with whatever he had in mind. We were adults and since we were married and expecting, I hardly can imagine that his parents thought we never had sex. It still felt weird. Except with Ramsey's seductive tactics, it was impossible to stop him, when he loved pleasing me so much.

We spent the next couple days doing things with his parents. They took the kids to the aquarium and came back with their hands full of presents. As for me and Ramsey, well, we spent the afternoon at the cemetery.

I was nervous going there. I just felt like it wasn't my place, but he insisted. Since it seemed so important to him, I agreed to go. The cemetery was actually beautiful. The landscaping and statues of angels made for a serene atmosphere. We walked down a little hill after we parked and came up to a small bench. He pointed to the two headstones across from it and I read the names. Then he took my hand and we both sat down. I had fresh flowers in my hand, but was afraid to make a move. Ramsey was so quiet. He sat still, just staring at the headstones. He kept my hand in his, sometimes rubbing mine with his thumb. I understood his silence, but it was hard to say nothing when I knew he was in pain.

Finally, after at least ten minutes, he just started talking. "Jules' parents put the bench in a couple months ago. They come here every Sunday."

"It's very pretty here."

"Yeah, I think so."

I put my arm around him. "Do you want me to give you a minute? I can go back to the car."

I didn't want him to feel like he couldn't say something because I was there. This was his own personal time with his girls. I knew how important it was.

He put his arm over my shoulder and pulled me closer, while kissing the top of my head. "There's nothing I have to say that you can't hear, Vessa. You being a part of this is important to me. They're my past, but you're my future. That's never going to change."

I smiled and leaned my head into him for a second. Without asking if it was okay, I walked up to Jules' stone. It was hard with my belly, but I knelt down in front of it and set up the flowers in the holder. "I promise to spend every day of my life taking care of him, Jules."

When I turned around to look, he was smiling with tears in his eyes. He mouthed the words 'thank you' and held out his hand to help me stand up. We stood there for a few more minutes, holding hands.

Once we set up Katie's flowers, we headed out and had lunch. A couple people recognized him and came over to say hello. He introduced me as his wife and told them about our life in West Virginia. I was surprised when the guy asked him if he still shot pool. He laughed and looked at me, before explaining that he married me to steal all of my skills.

When they finally walked away, he was all smiles. "Do you miss living here? We can move if you want. I mean, we could always sell the restaurant and buy another house."

"Vessa, I love where we live. I don't want you having to worry if I'm coming home at night, like I know Jules did. I don't miss the city life, at all. I like my job. It's easy and I can be with you whenever I need to be. My old station was constantly working on cases. I worked eight hours running around with criminals and putting my life on the line. We don't have that where we live. The kids can grow up and play outside without us having to be out there with them. That's the kind of life that I want for my family."

"I just want you to be happy. I feel like you've taken on my life and I don't want you to have to do that." I knew what it was like to be in a marriage where it was all about the other person. I couldn't take him ever resenting me.

"I'm the one that wanted to get married. It was my idea to fix up the restaurant. I love living in your aunt's old house. It's big enough for all of us and the property is fantastic. Would you stop with the worrying? I will be so glad when you pop out that kid and get back to being your spunky self."

"I worry too much."

"Yes, you do. Just relax and enjoy life with me. You never know what tomorrow brings and I will spend every minute of my life being happy. I've wasted away enough time."

"I really do love you, so much." He was everything I could have asked for in a man. "I even loved the stubborn hermit that you used to be."

He reached over the table and kissed me. "That's the nicest thing anyone has ever said to me. I love you too, honey. Now finish eating before the kids talk my parents into taking them to Disney World. I don't know which one of them is more excited about having each other. Did you see my parents light up earlier today? I told you that you had nothing to worry about. Everything is going to be alright." He sang like Bob Marley. I laughed and rolled my eyes.

When it was time to say goodbye, I felt like a weight had lifted off me. Ramsey had been right all along about his parents. They never made me feel like I was just a replacement. His mother was genuinely grateful that I'd pushed my way into her son's life. She didn't know that he'd pushed his way right inside of mine. At the end of the day, I was thrilled to have such considerate people to call family.

We were so blessed and seeing my kids so happy made me overjoyed.

Logan always called Ramsey his hero. He would always be my hero, too.

Epilogue

Ramsey

You're probably wondering who won the bet about naming the baby. We actually didn't get to play our match until a week before the baby was born. With the construction finished on the restaurant and everything else we had to do to get it going, by the time we got home at night we were both too tired to go downstairs and stand around.

Finally, on a Sunday morning, I found Vessa downstairs folding clothes. She insisted on doing the laundry, even when she couldn't carry up the baskets anymore. I tried to explain to her that I could wash clothes, but after she'd seen me attempt to cook some things, she decided that she was just going to do it.

That was the hardhead that I fell in love with.

When I started shooting balls around on the table, she came into the pool table area with her hands on her back. Her belly was so big that standing became a task on its own.

We'd talked about baby names, but each time, we went back to letting the game decide.

Vessa pointed to the rack that was hanging on the wall. "Are we starting over?"

"Of course. I'll even let you break."

She smiled and pulled her dad's old stick out of its case. I watched her chalking it up while making sure I didn't give her a loose rack to break up. It was kind of a way to cheat. The looser the rack, the harder it was to break out the balls. For a good player, the break was a big part of the strategy to run out the balls. If no balls were made, you lost your turn.

I started laughing when I saw her questioning me. "What? I was just making sure you weren't …"

"I see how you are. Break up the balls, woman."

She won the first rack easily, almost like she hadn't taken a day off from playing. That woman had skills—that was for sure. The second game consisted of a bunch of safety shots on both of us. I managed to win, barely. I broke and ran out the third game. She kicked my ass the fourth game. During the fifth game was when I saw her change her game. She started smiling and laughing when she missed. Finally, with her next turn, she got on the eight ball. "As soon as I make this, I can tell you the names I picked out," she teased.

I felt defeated.

Then she grabbed the cue ball and tossed it in a pocket, forfeiting and giving me the win. She giggled and walked up to kiss me. As her lips pulled away from mine, she opened her eyes. "I wanted you to win."

It was all about the hustle when it came to Vessa and the game of pool. Luckily, I finally got to be her partner on pool league nights. I'd much rather have her play with me instead of against me.

My son weighed nine pounds and nine ounces and took twenty hours of labor to finally come into the world. Vessa was a champ considering his size. She wasn't a happy camper trying to push him out though.

Mason Andrew Towers was welcomed into this world by his brother and sister and also my parents. Vessa had to be induced, so it gave them time to drive to town and look after the kids while I stayed at the hospital the whole time.

I can't explain the kind of emotions that I felt when the doctor put my son in my arms. I was already happy building a future with Vessa, but having a child that we made out of love, was the best kind of gift I could have ever received. I felt whole again, like my life had purpose. I was going to be good father; I already felt like I was to Vessa's children. It pained me to think back to a time where I didn't want to be surrounded by the people that cared about me. Looking around the room, at all of the people in my life, made me feel so thankful.

My parents only stayed for a week before heading back home. While they visited, we took them out and showed them our restaurant and where I worked.

Vessa fell right into taking care of a newborn. I guess it's like riding a bike.

I made the cover of the local paper again. This time the title read:

Sheriff And Wife Welcome Baby Boy.

It made me smile when Vessa hung it up on the refrigerator and the bulletin board at the restaurant.

I spent more time at home, only going out when there were important calls or situations that I had to tend to. Vessa liked me being there and spending most of my time with her and Mason. The truth was that I couldn't get enough of my son. He looked like me, except his dimples were huge. I knew it was just gas, but when he smiled, it made me smile.

One day we were lying on the bed while Vessa folded his little clothes. I was making raspberry sounds and sticking my face into his neck, playing. He was just drooling and being a baby, like every day. I guess he was about four to six weeks old. I kept tickling him and he wouldn't stop smiling. Vessa climbed on the bed with us. He saw her and smiled even more. "Look who is happy today," she said in a baby voice.

"I'm happy every day, "I jokingly replied.

She leaned over and pressed her lips against mine. "Me too."

"You think he's ready to learn how to play pool?"

She grabbed his little hands and made faces. "Daddy thinks he's going to teach you to play pool. Tell him Mommy's going to teach you." He kept smiling. "Tell him, big boy." I think she didn't even have to talk in a baby voice. He always responded to the sound of her talking.

"Fine! As long as I get to watch, then I'm alright with that."

She giggled and kissed me again. "Get him to take a nap and I'll shoot you without clothes on."

"Meet me downstairs in ten minutes." I picked up my son and took him to the nursery. It took about fifteen, but when I got down those steps and saw her laying there with nothing on, I knew it was going to be a good day.

This was our life. I never thought that something beautiful could come from something so devastating. It didn't matter how we got there. All that mattered was where we belonged.

The End!

Look For Book Seven in The Mitchell Family Series, Summer 2013 (Told by Colt and Savanna)

If you enjoyed this book, please share a comment or review.

Let me know what you think of this book by contacting me at the follow:

http://www.jenniferfoor.com

http://twitter.com/jennyfoor

http://www.facebook.com/#!/JenniferFoorAuthor

http://www.jennyfoor.wordpress.com

http://www.goodreads.com/jennyfoor

Jennifer Foor lives on the Eastern Shore of Maryland with her husband and two children. She enjoys shooting pool, camping and catching up on cliché movies that were made in the eighties.

www.ingramcontent.com/pod-product-compliance
Lightning Source LLC
Chambersburg PA
CBHW071126170626
46809CB00002B/506